BOOK TWO OF THE NEVERMORE TRILOGY

Bound (The Nevermore Trilogy, Book 2) Anniversary Edition

Published by HiJinks Ink LTD.
www.shannonmayer.com

Original Cover Art by Damon Za
Mayer, Shannon

Bound

BOOK TWO OF THE NEVERMORE TRILOGY

SHANNON MAYER

Also By Shannon Mayer

The Rylee Adamson Novels

Priceless (Book 1)
Immune (Book 2)
Raising Innocence (Book 3)
Shadowed Threads (Book 4)
Blind Salvage (Book 5)
Tracker (Book 6)
Veiled Threat (Book 7)
Wounded (Book 8)
Rising Darkness (Book 9)
Blood of the Lost (Book 10)
Alex (A Short Story)
Tracking Magic (A Novella 0.25)
Elementally Priceless (A Novella 0.5)
Guardian (A Novella 6.5)
Stitched (A Novella 8.5)

The Rylee Adamson Epilogues

RYLEE (Book 1)
LIAM (Book 2)
PAMELA (Book 3)

THE ELEMENTAL SERIES

Recurve (Book 1)
Breakwater (Book 2)
Firestorm (Book 3)
Windburn (Book 4)
Rootbound (Book 5)
Ash (Book 6)

THE VENOM TRILOGY

Venom & Vanilla (Book 1)
Fangs & Fennel (Book 2)
Hisses & Honey (Book 3)

THE BLOOD BORNE SERIES
(WRITTEN WITH DENISE GROVER SWANK)

Recombinant (Book 1)
Replica (Book 2)

THE NEVERMORE TRILOGY

Sundered (Book 1)
Bound (Book 2)
Dauntless (Book 3)

A Celtic Legacy

Dark Waters (Book 1)
Dark Isle (Book 2)
Dark Fae (Book 3)

The Risk Series
(Written as S.J. Mayer)

High Risk Love (Book 1)

Contemporary Romances
(Written as S.J. Mayer)

Of The Heart

BOUND

A man is not where he lives, but where he loves.

-Latin Proverb

Chapter One

Mara

There are moments in time that define you. Moments that make you who you are and force you to delve deep within your heart to grasp hold of the person you want to be. They are hard, gut-wrenching, soul-splitting seconds that leave us spiritually drained. Yet somehow in the end—if we let them—they can make us stronger.

The blade in my hand caught the sunlight, flickering a shimmer of rainbow as I brought it down. To kill him.

Sebastian. My husband. Lover. Father of my unborn child.

Nevermore.

He'd taken the Nevermore shot, a drug meant to heal, a drug that should have saved the world and cured so many diseases. Instead, it changed those who'd taken it, creating a new predator beyond deadly on the food chain.

They were intelligent, worked in packs like wolves. They had strength and speed. Wild and unpredictable.

And worst of all, they outnumbered those who hadn't taken the shot by ten to one.

Sebastian and I had been locked down on our rural farm since the outbreak, doing our best to survive behind a large gate with meager food supplies. We'd been doing okay, not great, but making it. Building something of a future.

Until the truth came out.

Sebastian, the love of my life, had taken the shot. He'd done it for us, so we could have a child. After his transformation, his love for me remained strong and he watched over me, keeping other creatures from hurting me and the unborn baby.

I had to believe our love held true, even now. If not, what was the point of going on?

The knife seemed frozen over Sebastian's back. A simple choice lay in front of me. Death or love?

I chose love.

My fingers released the smooth wooden handle and the blade fell to the dusty, hard-packed ground beside me.

"I can't, Sebastian. I can't kill you." Calm flooded me and soothed the fear away. I accepted there was a good chance he would kill me. That the pack he led would clean my bones and feed their young and old alike with my flesh. But I would trust whatever came. I would trust my heart.

He let out a long groan and his body sagged onto

mine as he pressed his face against my neck. Slowly his arms encircled me. He might have been different, changed. But he was now and forever my love.

He remembered me.

I clung to him, barely holding back the sobs that built in my chest. Before I could do anything more than hold him, Sebastian stood and pulled me to my feet alongside him.

He stepped back and lifted his hands to my face to wipe away the tears that streaked down and dripped off my chin.

A screech broke the silent air around us. We whipped around and stared down the long curving road.

Reality crashed around us. We might have found peace between us, but the rest of the Nevermore pack was not going to allow Sebastian to leave. One female in particular was out for my blood because she knew Sebastian had been mine. Was still mine.

In other words, I had to get on my side of the gate before the rest of the pack showed up.

I turned, sliding my hands off Sebastian's hard body. "I have to go. They can't catch me outside the fence. You can't protect me from all of them."

He nodded and lifted his eyes toward the gate.

There was a bark from the other side and then a pained cry.

"Missy?"

Sebastian let out a growl, his lips rippling with the noise.

The gate swung open, and a man stepped onto the road. He wore army fatigues, dark sunglasses, and a baseball cap. I took it all in, in an instant.

My eyes rested on the rather large gun he had pointed at us. If I were to guess, I would say it was an assault rifle with far more power than the simple rifle sitting on the table in the farmhouse. His thumb flicked over the gun and there was a click that seemed to echo.

"Lady, step away from the Nevermore. Slowly with no quick movements. It draws their attention."

I put my hands up and moved to stand between Sebastian and the army dude. This was what Dan had said was happening—the military was moving in. I just didn't think it would be so quick. But where was Dan? Had he called these men in? If so, he should be here.

Unless he didn't trust the army, either.

"No, you don't understand. He's not like the others."

Sebastian let out a snarl and leapt past me. Of course, he only saw the threat to me, a threat that had to be annihilated.

"No!" I ran after him but was unable to keep up with his speed.

A boom rattled the world around us and Sebastian's body jerked backward. A bloom of red spread out of his back. His right shoulder was covered in blood, like a splatter paint show gone horribly wrong.

I let out a cry as if the bullet had gone through me

and not him. This couldn't be happening, not now, not when we were so close to being safe.

Another ungodly howl went up from down the road, and I heard the Nevermores running, their feet beating a discordant tempo on the dirt-packed road.

"Lady, you need to get behind this gate. Now," Mr. Army said.

I ignored him and dropped to the ground next to Sebastian. He was on his hands and knees, panting hard. Blood dripped from the gunshot wounds as well as his mouth. Did that mean the bullet had hit his lung?

"Shut the hell up and help me!" I snapped at Mr. Army. I tried with little success to lift Sebastian. Even with his diminished body fat, his size made it nearly impossible for me to pick him up. The Nevermores were, if nothing else, solid brick shithouses.

I looked up at the hard line of Mr. Army's mouth. "I mean it, asshole. Help me get him up and inside that gate now!"

Sebastian growled, low and seriously pissed. I shushed him. "Be quiet, he's going to help." Mr. Army drew closer, his eyebrows raised above his sunglasses. His gun did not lower once.

"He's one of them."

"No, he's not." I glared at him. "Either you help me help him, or we'll stay out here together."

"Fuck it all," Mr. Army snapped. "God save me from the bleeding hearts."

Sebastian gave up on the growling and focused on just breathing.

Mr. Army moved to Sebastian's other side. He slung the gun over one shoulder and helped Sebastian to his feet.

"Heavy-ass monsters. It's like they eat lead for breakfast."

I ignored him. My only concern was getting Sebastian somewhere safe. The scent of blood and his diminished ability to protect himself would make him the pack's next meal. I was not letting that happen.

We hustled to the gate and pulled Sebastian through just as the pack thundered up behind us. They hollered and screamed and beat their fists on the metal bars.

Jessica was the worst of the bunch. She yanked her own hair and hit other pack members around her if they got too close. She was pissed, to say the least. I gave her a little wave.

Sebastian groaned and his whole body shook. My attention came back to him.

"We've got to get him inside the house. I have to get that wound clean."

A second man, one I also didn't know, answered me. "You are out of your mind, lady. This big bastard is going to tear us all apart. Step away from him now."

I looked up and sucked in a sharp breath. Sebastian slumped against me, and I struggled to hold him upright while staring at the scene in front of me. A large dark green army vehicle sat in our driveway, looming over us. Two large machine guns were attached to the front, and blood splattered the grill and hood. The men who surrounded it wore fatigues. And they had guns leveled at us. There was no way they would give him a chance if he so much as twitched.

One of them held a rope to a straining Missy. Her eyes were on mine. She knew we were in trouble. Nero paced beside her. At almost five months old, he was a big boy, but still kind of a mush. I held a hand out to her and she sat. Even so, her body shook with the effort to do as I asked.

"As soon as she is clear, shoot him."

The words stole the air from my lungs.

The men lifted their guns.

I twisted so my body was between them and Sebastian.

"You will *not* shoot my husband. What the hell are you doing here? On my—our—property. We don't want your kind of help." I tightened my grip around Sebastian's waist, doing my best to look over my shoulder at the military men. How was I going to protect Sebastian? I couldn't blame them, not really. He *was* one of the monsters.

But at the moment, he was pretty much harmless, and even without the injury, I was sure he would listen to me. I was sure he wouldn't hurt them if I asked him not to. His head lolled to my shoulder and he slid almost to his knees. Mr. Army who'd helped us get inside the gate moved to stand with his men near the hulking vehicle. I shifted my arms again and struggled to hold Sebastian upright on my own.

Mr. Army held his gun across his body. "Stand down, men. We aren't shooting a human, even if she is being an idiot."

I glared at him, awkward over my shoulder, but I did it.

With a smattering of clicks, the guns lowered one by one. He went on to answer, at least, some of my questions. "Our satellite photos show this region as being one of the least infected areas, which means it also has the highest possibility of survivors." His voice was perfectly even, and his expression unreadable behind the dark glasses and cap.

"And how many humans have you found alive?" I wanted to know, because other than Dan and the four raiders, I'd seen nothing in the almost three months since the world fell apart.

No answer from him was answer enough. None. He'd found none. Being rural had nothing to do with being safe. Anywhere there were people, they'd taken the shot. End of story in the most literal of senses.

Sebastian slid to the ground and I followed him. I wasn't letting him go now. With my arms around him as best I could, I waited for what would come.

Two men strode forward with their guns trained on Sebastian and me. A third man in crisp, neatly pressed army fatigues followed more slowly. He had a gun on either side of his waist like an old-school gunslinger. But it was the large bobby stick he held in his one hand and repeatedly thumped into the palm of the other that kept my attention. He only stopped when he stood over us, guns at his waist and stick in his hand. A cruel twist to his thin lips made me wonder if he enjoyed all the killing.

"You must be Mara, and I assume this is your Sebastian?" His voice was icy cold.

"How do you know who I am?" I began to shake from exertion, exhaustion, and the loss of adrenaline pumping through me.

He arched an eyebrow, tucked his hands behind his back and bent at the waist. That same cruel smile stayed on his mouth the entire time.

I wouldn't have been shocked to see "bad guy" printed on his army tags.

"We've searched your house," he said. "Confiscated your food. Through the search, we found your information. Though Sebastian here looks rather different from your wedding pictures. Obviously, it is still him." His eyes narrowed and he tipped his head to one side. "Amazing that there is somehow a connection between the two of you, despite the Nevermore drug." He leaned closer toward Sebastian, and my husband let out a low growl. I put my hand over his mouth. This man standing over us . . . I had no doubt he would kill us both without remorse.

I swallowed hard. "Who are you and what do you want from us?"

"I'm Vincent and these are my men, what's left of the local army." He patted his bobby stick against his thigh. "How is it that he doesn't try to eat you? What training methods did you use? Torture?" Something dark, an emotion I couldn't put my finger on, flickered through his eyes as he spoke. He blinked once, twice, and then shook himself out of wherever his thoughts had taken him.

"I didn't train him. He loves me."

He snorted. "Bullshit." His eyes flared with anger and then emptied of any emotion. "You're coming with us, Mara. For now, you can keep your pet monster."

That was it. No explanation as to why he would keep Sebastian alive. Nothing.

Hands latched on to my arms and dragged me toward the truck. I kicked and screamed, no longer caring if the Nevermores heard me. Sebastian made a feeble lunge, but he was weak from his wound, too weak to do anything but growl and snap his teeth.

The men laughed and made rude gestures at me. Several of them thrust their hips in my direction. "Can't believe we got another woman," one of them said.

I truly hoped I was misinterpreting, but I knew that was a joke. These men were their own breed of animals. I fought harder, kicking and jerking my body from side to side. "Let me go!"

"No, you are army property now, Mara," Vincent said. "Get used to it. You belong to me."

My breath came in ragged gasps and the skin on my arms burned where the men's fingers dug into my flesh.

Finally, they let me go, but it was only to watch me fall to my knees. I hit the ground hard. Missy barked and lunged toward me. Nero let out a whine. I held my hand out to them again. The last thing I wanted was for the dogs to get hurt trying to protect me. There was nothing that Missy or Nero could do to help us out of this any more than I could.

The men laughed at me. "Ah, look, she's trying to protect her doggies. How cute."

"Obviously, she's an animal lover. Look at what she's been fucking." More laughter.

Tears of anger burned the back of my eyes. I held them in. I would not cry in front of these asshats.

Black army boots came into view and I looked up. Mr. Army himself stood in front of me. "You're making this harder than it has to be. And I would think the condition you're in, that's the last thing you'd want to do." He made a small motion towards my baby bump.

His eyes softened only a little, but I realized that he was in his own way trying to help me. How he knew I was pregnant I could only guess.

I pulled in a deep breath and the scent of the cracked earth and the dry air filled my nose, tickling it. I let out a sneeze that I tried to keep in and failed, which resulted in a high-pitched squeaking noise.

"Oh, isn't that cute. She's a damn mouse when she wants to be," one of the men said in a high falsetto, which sent the men into another bout of laughter. Mr. Army stepped forward and offered me his hand, well-worn and callused. I stared at it, took stock of the bruises and aches throughout my body and let go of my pride. If I needed anything right now, it was an ally. A friend.

I took the offered hand and the men around us

immediately began to catcall and whistle. As soon as I had my feet under me, I snatched my hand back.

With a single snap of his fingers, Mr. Army silenced the men, his voice once more hard and in control without a hint of the compassion he'd shown me.

"Get the big bastard loaded up. It's time to leave."

CHAPTER TWO

Sebastian

Images flashed through my mind, fast and furious, as my pack edged around the gate behind me.

What is happening?

Is the Alpha dead?

Do we leave him?

Do we fight?

Hunger.

Anger.

Confusion.

Fear.

They were afraid for me, afraid for the very reason I'd wanted Mara to kill me. Without a leader, they would struggle to survive. One of the other packs might take them over, but more likely they would all be slaughtered. Eaten. Or at least the males would be. The females would be kept as breeders.

I sent back an image, the only thing I could do.

Stay and let Fire—Jessica—lead the pack. The images of confusion, scattered and disorienting, rushed through me and made my head spin.

I let out a low growl directed at the pack and a man cuffed my head. "Shut your mouth."

I didn't look at him. I locked eyes with Scout and sent a series of quick images to him and only him.

Hide under the truck. Come with us. Protect my mate.

He gave a tight nod and slid to the side of the gate, into the shadows we both knew so well. The rest of the pack began to withdraw, following Jessica into the bush. They would do as I commanded for now, but I didn't know if it would last. A part of me still wanted to protect them, to make sure they survived.

They were a part of my life.

But Mara was my heart, and I would go with her wherever she led.

I looked at the hulking vehicle. Beside it Mara stood with her hand in that of a stranger's. A man. I let out another low growl and lurched forward.

Hands gripped my upper arms and lifted me toward the truck.

"Shit, he's heavy."

"You know they all are. Their bones are denser. That's what the doc already said."

Doc. Doctor? Warmth trickled down my side from the gunshot wound and my mind slipped a little into the wildness of the Nevermore drug. I jerked hard to one side and pulled the two men with me.

They grunted and went with me as we tussled.

Cold metal clamped onto my wrists and my hands were locked behind my back. I lunged again, and snapped my teeth at the man closest to me. I caught the edge of his jacket. His eyes widened and the pupils dilated. A faint scent of urine rose up around him. I yanked him toward me. If I could get my mouth on his neck I could—

Something slammed into the back of my head and darkness swallowed me in a single explosion of pain.

CHAPTER THREE

Mara

Men rushed forward and secured Sebastian's hands behind his back with a large set of handcuffs. They dragged him to the back of the large truck. He snarled and the men holding him tried to wrestle him into submission.

He grabbed the man closest to him with his teeth, and one of the other men behind Bastian slammed the butt of his gun into his head, silencing him.

"Don't hurt him!" I struggled to free my hands from Mr. Army. Behind me, the pack howled as though Bastian's pain was theirs. Nero could stand it no longer. He ran for me, the two men who'd been standing beside him belatedly leaping to stop him. One of them looked as though he was barely old enough to shave.

I whistled and Nero ran straight to me. Big as he was, when he leapt for me we tumbled to the ground.

I held him tightly. I wouldn't cry in front of these men, they weren't worth my tears or emotions. Missy strained at her makeshift leash, whimpering and diving against it.

"You can't bring two dogs with you; we've got enough trouble feeding ourselves without adding a mutt to the mix," Vincent said.

"I'll feed them off my own plate. I'm not leaving either of them behind."

"I'm not giving you a choice," Vincent snapped. "The bitch has some good training. The pup is useless. We don't do useless." He reached out and snatched Nero from my arms by the scruff of his neck. He had to drag him because Nero wasn't going without a fight. He squirmed and cried out, then finally tried to bite Vincent. At his age, he was already a solid fifty-pound dog and he made Vincent fight for every step.

"Stop! Give him back! You asshole!" I lunged for him.

Vincent smirked at my attempt even as sweat rolled down his face. He bent and got his arms under Nero's middle and benched him over his head.

I screamed; Missy's cry echoed mine.

Vincent heaved Nero over the gate. The pack who'd been retreating paused and spun.

Food had been dropped onto their side of the gate.

"Run, Nero, run!" I lurched forward, knowing that there was nothing I could do. There were too many against us.

Nero yelped as he hit the ground. He got to his feet and seemed to realize the trouble he was in. Scout leapt out from the shadows and snarled at the pup, driving Nero up the road.

He was a blur of yellow gold. The majority of the pack chased him up the road, a howling mass of hunger.

The steady thump of feet rolled back to us, then a high-pitched cry, and finally, silence.

Tears streaked my face.

I spun and punched Vincent as hard as I could. My knuckles popped as my fist connected squarely with his jaw. He stumbled back, tripped on a piece of wood, and fell on his butt.

"You're a piece of shit." I lifted a foot to kick him while he was down. He deserved no less.

Silence fell over us for a brief second as I booted at Vincent and he rolled to avoid me.

Vincent glared up at me, his eyes full of hatred as he caught my next kick in mid-air. He twisted my leg and sent me to the ground in a hard fall. I managed to land on my hip but that was a small comfort.

Vincent stood and loomed over me, his hand twitching over the gun at his side. Every move screamed he was barely controlling his anger. Barely.

"Clark," he motioned Mr. Army over. "Get everyone else on the truck. We've got to head back with the supplies and the prisoners."

Clark nodded, saluted, and started to shout orders.

"You'll pay for that," Vincent said, as he dusted his pants off. "This is not the world you remember. You have no rights. You are our property now."

"Bring it, bitch," I snarled at him. There was no

way Nero would survive out there, not with the pack and Bob the bear on the loose.

Missy was handed to me by the young kid. He wouldn't meet my eyes.

Vincent walked away and all I could think about was the rifle. If I had it with me then, I would have shot him without a single bit of remorse.

"Get her in the truck!" Clark snapped and the men jumped, hustling me to the back of the army vehicle. I pulled my arms free of the men escorting me, though; I suppose they let me go. I was shoved next to Sebastian behind the cab of the truck. Missy leapt in, but her eyes searched the farm. Searched for her baby.

I bit down on my lips to keep the tears in. Missy whined softly and then sat. But she didn't stop looking out.

The other men settled into the back of the truck, a few feet away from the three of us. That was fine by me. I pulled Bastian's head into my lap and pressed my hand against the gunshot wound, applying pressure as best I could. He let out a low moan, and I whispered soft nothings to him. The sound of my voice seemed to keep him calm. The last thing I needed was for him to give these men a reason to hurt him more. Or worse, kill him outright.

Clark jumped into the back of the truck and dropped the canvas flap. One last glimpse of our farm, and then it was gone.

I had no illusions that we'd see our home again.

Clark stared at me and Sebastian, a look of derision evident on his face.

"What's it like having sex with a monster?" he asked, his lips curled with disdain.

So that was how it was going to be? Fine. I could give it as good as anyone.

"I don't know. Why don't you ask your father?" I held Sebastian close, still keeping pressure on the wound.

There was dead silence for a split second. Then the laughter started as the other men guffawed at Clark's expense, the noise quickly filling the back of the truck.

"She got you there, Clark."

"Damn, that's some sass for a woman this far out. You remember the last gal we brought in? Pulled most of her hair out . . ."

"Not to mention she was a raving lunatic."

"What was it she said was stuck in her head?"

"Bees, she was screaming about bees in her head she couldn't get out." Laughter rippled around the truck again and I ignored it, focusing on the fact that Sebastian was still breathing, slow and steady, the blood clotting on his chest wound.

Missy sat herself between me and the men. Every time one of them moved she lifted her lips and showed her teeth.

Good. I didn't want her liking any of them. They were in their own way as bad as the Nevermores we'd had to deal with the last few months.

"Don't worry about him," a new voice said. I glanced over my shoulder; it was the young man who'd been chasing Nero.

"I'm Green, by the way. Sergeant Green. I was

looking after your dogs for you," he said, his words sincere, his face open and very honest looking.

I didn't want to like him. I didn't want to like any of them. Not when I already knew they saw me as property and Sebastian as something to be disposed of.

I glared at him. "You didn't do a very good job, did you?"

Green had the decency to blush and duck his head.

"I didn't expect him to run away from his mom. I'm sorry," he said.

I was surprised by his apology. "Thank you."

"Don't apologize to the prisoners, Green," Clark snapped.

Green retreated and I went back to crooning to Sebastian, singing softly. I didn't bother to ask where we were going. It didn't really matter. We were captives, trapped, and God only knew what was going to happen to us when we got to where we were going.

The only good thing was that Sebastian and I were together. We had Missy, and we had each other.

I wondered how long it would last. Would we be separated? Would Missy find herself thrown to the Nevermores as Nero had been? The thought gutted me. I reached out and touched her back. She looked at me, and if I didn't know better, I'd say tears tracked down her golden cheeks. I had to look away, my own emotions rising with the vision of grief she presented.

I would not cry in front of these men. I refused to.

A half hour into our drive, the truck slowed and I thought we'd arrived at our destination. Maybe they'd taken us to Comox and the air force bunkers there. That was a possibility, and the timing was right.

Sebastian stirred and groaned softly. A word, a human word, slipped over his lips.

"Nevermores."

A subtle screech of nails on metal and a scream of rage from outside the truck lit the air.

Clawed, dusky yellow hands shot into the back of the moving truck. The canvas flap was jerked to the side.

Nevermores ran behind and next to the truck. Their eyes were rage filled, their bodies lean and their intention obvious. We had a currently slow-moving wagon full of food.

They howled as they leapt and tried to get into the back.

I tried to drag Sebastian to away from the back but I couldn't move him. A Nevermore hooked his arms over the edge of the tailgate and half pulled himself in. The men seemed frozen. I had no doubt they would not save me or Sebastian.

I pulled the rope off Missy.

"Missy, get him!"

She shot forward and bit the Nevermore on the arm closest to her. He screeched and let go. A clawed hand reached for her, but she dodged him easily. She knew what she was up against.

I snapped my fingers and she hurried back to me. I pulled her into a hug. "Good girl."

She licked my face, seemed to consider it a moment, and then licked Sebastian's face.

I scrunched up tightly against the two of them.

The men finally snapped out of their stupor. Two pulled back the canvas flap, revealing the mass behind us. Clark lifted his gun. "Shoot them all."

They open fired on the Nevermores.

The percussion of all those weapons in a small space was literally deafening. I clamped my hands over my ears, Missy and Sebastian buried their heads against my body.

The truck rocked hard to the side as a bunch of somethings slammed into it. The sound was like the pattering of rain, only the rain was hands as they hit in rapid succession on the metal. The truck engine groaned and there was a moment where the wheels on that side lifted.

"Over here," Clark directed, and everyone ran to that side of the truck, giving it weight.

I wasn't sure it would be enough.

When it came to food, I knew all too well how far a pack would go. And we were in their territory, all but waving the come-and-get-it flag.

The tension rose and the truck fell onto all four tires. Before the Nevermores could hit again, Clark slammed his hand on the back of the cab.

"Move it, dumbass!"

A second slam, that strange pattering of hands hitting one after another, rocked the vehicle as the driver found the gas pedal. We shot forward, leaving behind the screech of clawed fingers on the metal.

I let out a breath I didn't realize I'd been holding.

"Stand down. We don't need to draw more attention to us," Clark said.

A little too late, though.

A yellowed hand shot into the back of the truck. Like a strike of lightning, the hand closed over one of the men's ankles and yanked him out through the canvas material of the back flap. There was a single scream, and then nothing.

I bit the inside of my cheek to keep from screaming at the other men to do something. The noise would only add to the chaos.

The truck never slowed and the other men barely reacted other than to step farther away from the tailgate. We crowded toward the front of the truck, silent.

I looked at their faces, one by one, while they watched the canvas material flapping.

There was no sadness, no surprise, no grief.

They didn't look out for their own.

Sebastian, Missy, and I were in even more trouble than I'd thought. A part of me had hoped maybe with more people, more humans, we would be safer. That maybe first impressions had been shitty, but would get better.

Whatever hopes I'd had fell out of the back of the truck along with the soldier.

Silence surrounded the truck as quickly as the Nevermores had. The pack that had chased us gave up on their quest. They'd snagged their prize. A meal in the form of one unsuspecting man.

I pressed my face against Sebastian's and took slow

even breaths. There was no way I could do this without him, even though so much of who he had been was lost. Missy burrowed her face beside ours.

"Hang on, love," I whispered. "Just hang on."

CHAPTER FOUR

Sebastian

Mara's words rolled through me. Hang on.

The Nevermores who'd attacked the truck had been starving. There was nothing left in their area that was easy access and their Alpha had been killed. Part of the reason they'd attacked the truck had nothing to do with food.

They'd sensed me inside. An Alpha. Injured. But still I could have led them. Could have given them purpose. I frowned and pressed my face against Mara's chest. No, I was not a monster, I was . . . was Mara's. Just that. Just here.

The Nevermores would survive without me, I knew that. They—I—were still learning what it meant to be this wild creature. Every day new understandings came to me, new growth. Understanding that this was Mother Nature's way of evening things out, of making the humans left behind stronger. Only those worthy would survive this new world. I knew it. That truth went for both the Nevermore and the humans.

Maybe something bad was coming, something worse than packs of monsters that roved with an insatiable hunger. I snorted softly and then groaned. The wound in my side was healing, but it hurt when I moved too quickly.

The dog . . . she stared into my eyes. I stared back, not sure why she suddenly let me so close to Mara. She sneezed and shook her head, and for just a moment, I thought . . . I thought I saw what she thought. A simple thing.

Mara was all she had left. Mara was her pack. And maybe . . . maybe I was, too.

CHAPTER FIVE

Mara

"We're here." Clark stood and slung his gun around. The men scrambled to their feet and moved to the back of the truck. From outside, there was the click of a lock unfastening, and a large gate rattling open, then the sounds reversed as the gate was shoved closed. Presumably behind the truck.

The trip had taken a little over an hour, and I still didn't know if we'd gone south, east or west. Those were the only options, seeing as the water was to the north. I dared a look at Sebastian's wound. I ran a finger over the spot where the bullet had gone in. The opening was barely even a quarter inch across now.

Clark pushed back the flap cover of the truck with the tip of his gun, drawing my eyes to him. So maybe he wasn't sure things were safe either. One of the other men jumped out and tied the canvas back to one side. Bright sunlight flooded in and blinded me. After the dim gray interior of the truck, my eyes did not want to adjust. Hands grabbed at me and pulled me out. Missy growled and I snapped my fingers. "With me, Missy."

She leapt out. I heard the sound of her nails on the truck bed as she kicked off.

Sebastian grunted. I spun to see him struggling to stay with me. One of the remaining men reached for him. Bastian snapped at the man. He was only trying to get to me, I knew that. But they didn't.

The distinct thud of a rifle butt as it slammed into a skull resounded in the still air.

"Stop hitting him!" I twisted hard and tried to free myself from the hands that gripped me.

Missy whined, but I snapped my fingers again, stopping her from moving away from my side. The last thing I needed was to lose her. I had no doubt it wouldn't take much to decide the dog was not worth the trouble.

I, on the other hand, was not going down without a fight and they were still hitting him.

"Stop it. He's quiet!" I managed to get one hand free and reach for Bastian. He lifted his hand and clamped his fingers around me. Now that was a surprise. Not that he reached for me. But the mobility of his fingers, the dexterity had improved tenfold.

Were the Nevermores evolving still?

I wasn't sure if that was a good thing or not.

Vincent strode around the side of the truck. He watched everything that was happening with a gun held loosely in his hand. I had no doubt he would use it as casually as pointing his finger at someone. "Those bastards heal faster than any human; he won't even have the gunshot wound to worry about in a couple hours."

"Where are we?" I asked. Maybe I could keep their attention on me and away from Sebastian. But the question had merit, too. If we were going to escape, I needed to know where we were. I could see trees, a tall fence with razor wire around the top and some sort of wooden buildings that could be barracks. On three sides of the fence were several packs of Nevermores. They kept their distance but were well within sight.

In reality, this place—wherever it was—was no different than the farm. The Nevermores were there, waiting for their next meal to step outside the fence. I shivered. There had been moments on the ride here I'd convinced myself it would be better, safer, wherever the soldiers were taking us.

I turned a full circle and found myself staring across the water of the Georgia Straight and what was left of downtown Nanaimo, one of the major cities on Vancouver Island. That is if you considered a population of eighty thousand people major.

"The Diefenbaker bunker," Clark answered my question as he put his hand on my arm again. His fingers dug into my skin as he yanked me away from Sebastian.

Bastian looked up and I shook my head. "I'm okay. I'll find you."

That would have to be enough. *God let me find a way out of this place for us.* Missy was all but glued to my side as Clark dragged me along. I wasn't fighting him, but I wasn't making it easy, either.

One of the small sheds loomed in front of us. Though it was *small*, I knew a prison when I saw one. I twisted around to see the other men dragging Sebastian in the opposite direction toward a door that rose out of a mound in the hill. That had to be the bunker. But why would they take Bastian into the bunker itself? Unless they were going to kill him the second we were separated.

I cradled my belly with one hand and tried to pull myself free. "Don't separate us. Please," I said. "I'm pregnant; I don't want to stress the baby." I looked into Clark's face and saw the softening I'd hoped for. Maybe he didn't like the fact that Sebastian was a Nevermore, but he didn't seem to be a complete ass. There had been moments that made me think perhaps I could turn him into an ally.

He paused and turned back. "Vincent. We can leave them together. If he kills her, it's one less mouth to feed."

Vincent frowned, but then a slow smile made its way across his face. There was no doubt in my mind that I was about to pay for humiliating him in front of his men. He motioned to Clark.

"Take her to the upper barracks; we don't have room in the bunker at the moment. And her *man* will be waiting for her when we do have room. If he behaves, that is." Vincent pointed to the wooden structures that Clark had first been dragging me to. He let out a low sigh and started toward the buildings once more.

"Thank you for trying." I needed him on my side. No matter what, I needed him to help me. Me and Sebastian.

He said nothing.

Clark put me in the first barracks and shut the door.

"Some advice for you, Mara. Don't piss him off. Vincent is not the kind of man you want to take on. He will destroy everything you love just to make a point. Do you understand?" He looked at me through a two-inch slatted opening at eye level in the door.

I nodded, frustration and fear chasing one another through me like a wicked game of cat and mouse. "Thanks for the warning, Clark. But I can't promise anything. I'm not backing down from him."

"I didn't think so," he muttered.

The lock clicked, the sound of retreating feet, and then I was alone.

I frowned and rubbed my hands over my face. These men held not only my life in their hands, but Sebastian's and Missy's, too. I would have to do my best to behave to get close to Bastian again. Missy whined softly.

"I know, I know. This is shitty."

I walked to the window and saw Sebastian being dragged to a large grass-covered mound. A flurry of activity and then the mound opened. A doorway leading into what I assumed was the bunker closed after they entered.

I looked over my room. Sparse was an understatement. There was a small cot with a thin blanket. That was it. Cement floors and a barred window with no glass. The hut was made of solid wood paneling that, as I tapped it, told me just how solid it was. No rot anywhere. "Damn it, this is not going to be easy to get out of."

I said the words and then really considered what I was saying. Did I actually think I could get the three of us out of here? I couldn't even stop Vincent from throwing Nero over the fence. My heart ached with his loss, knowing his death would have been anything but gentle.

I placed my hands on the bars. The cold and slightly rusted metal gave me a grounding sensation. We were surrounded by armed men who were some sort of militia. I didn't believe for a second that they were all ex-army. These were men who'd been gathered in the hunt for survivors. Green was a perfect example. He'd been kind and uncertain. Not things I'd ever associate with someone who'd been trained to go to war.

I tallied the obstacles we faced in my head. The men had guns and weapons. There was an enormous fence with razor wire on top, so no climbing. At least three Nevermore packs waited outside the fence. Finally, and this was the nail in the coffin . . . there was no way of knowing where we would even go from here. Back to the farm? Should we head south on the island or try and brave the strait that would take us to the mainland?

Tears threatened at the ridiculousness of the situation, but I pushed them back, swallowing the thickness that tightened my throat. Poor Nero was dead,

Sebastian was locked away from me, wounded and alone, and there wasn't a damn thing I could do about any of it. I hiccupped a sob back. Crying wouldn't do me any good, and I dashed the tears from my cheeks.

I blinked away the mist filming over my eyes and stared out the window, not sure if what I was seeing was a hallucination or reality.

From underneath the army truck we'd ridden in, a familiar figure dropped to the ground. He scuttled along the grass, lifting his face every once in a while to scent the air. Following his nose took him straight to the window I stared out of. He stood, smiling at me from the other side, his scrawny body battered from the ride he'd endured in the undercarriage of the truck. The dusky yellow skin was splattered here and there with brilliant pops of scarlet from tiny wounds all over his body.

Apparently Sebastian and I had inspired some serious loyalty in the pack. Or had Sebastian told Scout to follow us? Either way, we had some outside help, and that was all that mattered.

I smiled and gripped the bars of the window. He sniffed my fingers, but didn't try to bite me.

"Scout, how the hell are we going to get out of this mess?"

Chapter Six

Sebastian

Half dazed from the blow to my head, I barely noticed where the men dragged me. The bright sunlight disappeared and the air went from clear and fresh to that of stale bodies and fear. My eyes fluttered open as I fought the nausea that rolled through me.

"Damn, he's a big bastard," one of the men muttered.

"Stop bitching and keep moving. We need to get him into a cell before he wakes up."

"He didn't seem so bad."

"'Cause his wife was there with him."

They were quiet for a few minutes as they dragged me through the different hallways. I could find my way out if I needed to just by following the different smells. I didn't need to know exactly where the turns were or where they took me.

Their hands released me as they pushed me hard.

I went to my knees. My side ached and I struggled to my feet. Slowly, I turned to face the one man outside my cell. He stood three feet back from the bars.

Sweat trickled down his face into the grubby collar of his shirt. I didn't look away from him. "You can't get me from there."

I just stared.

"Why . . . didn't you attack your wife? My brother attacked me."

I frowned, not understanding what his brother had to do with anything. And I didn't particularly want to have a conversation with this man who'd imprisoned me.

"You think you love her more than my brother loved me?"

Again, I struggled to understand why my connection to Mara meant anything to him. A flicker of images floated to me. There were other Nevermores down here under the ground, trapped like I was. I focused on those instead of the human.

Curiosity was the strongest sensation that flowed from the Nevermores, followed closely by hunger. I closed my eyes, for the first time noticing that the raging hunger had eased in my gut. Maybe with everything else, it had finally given up? That was . . . interesting. And that fact alone, that I found something interesting outside of my base desires was . . . interesting.

A loud clanging snapped my eyes open. The man had approached the cage he'd stuffed me in and banged the metal bars with a baton. "Hey, I know you can talk. I heard you in the truck."

I shrugged and stepped into the shadows. A word here and there was hardly talking. Even I knew that.

"I have to stay down here with you." He backed up and grabbed a three-legged stool. He sat and stared at me. "My name is Green. My brother took the shot and when he turned into a Nevermore he tried to eat me. You have a name, don't you?"

I stared at him from the darkness. Names were things the humans did. Mara called me a name . . . I dredged it up from the depths of my memories. "Bastian."

He leapt from his stool. "I knew it. You can talk! How come you can talk and the others can't? Are you special? Did you get the shot before everyone else when the ingredients were still pure?"

His words battered against my aching head. I wanted him to shut up. I let out a low growl and the Nevermores around me echoed my sentiments. Green went to his stool again, eyes wide as he stared around.

"Look, I'm . . . I just am hoping maybe my brother can be helped, you know? He's still out there. He's still—"

"You don't really think you'll get them to talk, do you?"

That voice was the one of the man Mara had attacked. The one who threw the young dog over the fence. I stood and walked to the front of my cage. If I could get my hands on him, I was sure I could strangle him.

It was just a matter of waiting for the right moment.

"Vincent, he was *talking.* He said his name. I know you don't think Doc can do much, but maybe if we get Sebastian to him, they can find a cure."

"No such thing as a cure for something like this." Vincent spoke to Green while he stared at me. "You see, once you're a monster, there is no going back. I should know. I loved a woman who took the shot. We all knew people who took the shot. None of them come back." He paused and leaned a little closer to me. My fingers twitched. Patience, I needed to just have a little patience. "This one here is an anomaly. That much is obvious."

Green looked at Vincent, to Sebastian, and back again to Vincent. "I know that Doc—"

"Do not mention him again if you value your position here," Vincent said softly. A dangerous tone lit the words. His attention was on the boy. This was my chance.

I shot a hand through the bars.

I caught the edge of Vincent's shirt and yanked him toward me. He grunted as I slammed his back against the bars, smashing him hard. Green grabbed at Vincent and pulled him away from the cage.

I smiled at him, and slowly slid into the dark corner of my cage. "Lucky."

"Did you hear that?" Green whispered.

Vincent stood and put a hand to the back of his head. I already knew what he'd find, I smelled it.

His fingers came away red with his own blood. "If I didn't think I could still use him, I'd kill him now."

"Use him?" Green asked, but Vincent didn't answer that question.

"Feed the animals, *Private* Green. And try not to get bitten in the process. When you're done with them, feed the woman."

Green's face tightened. I noticed that Vincent called him a private. Had he just knocked him down a peg from his sergeant status?

Vincent's footsteps faded and Green stood unmoving until the sound of an upper doorway slammed shut. He snorted. "This from the idiot who puts his back to a Nevermore."

I smiled to myself. I didn't want to like Green. But he was making it difficult. And he was going to see Mara.

I made myself speak to him again. "Mara. Help. Mara."

Green stared at me and he shook his head. "I don't know."

"Help Mara." I bit the words out, struggling until I could get the last one to pass my lips.

"Please."

CHAPTER SEVEN

*M*ara

Scout smiled back at me, and chattered his teeth.

"Okay, you're excited. I get it." I had to fight not to pull my hands away from the bars. They were right next to his mouth, but he didn't seem inclined to bite.

He froze where he was, then spun. What had he heard? He tapped on my hand that gripped the bar, then scurried off around the side of the building to hide. A moment later, the mound where Sebastian had been taken opened and people poured out of the bunker. No, not just people. All men, all holding guns except Vincent.

The men lined up, rifles loose and at the ready. The last out of the bunker was . . . a woman. She was dragged forward and tied to a post against the high fence.

"You'll all rot in hell!" she screamed, and the Nevermores at the fence added their cries to hers.

Vincent held up a piece of paper. "For attempting to injure an officer of the Canadian army, you've been sentenced to death."

"They wouldn't," I whispered and glanced at Missy. "That's not even a real rule. There is no way that is in the rule books. He's making shit up." I shouldn't have been surprised, but I was.

Vincent folded up the bogus piece of paper. "Men."

The men raised their rifles. Horrified, I stood there. They weren't really going to do this. A heartbeat and the tension rose. "Aim." The word floated across the air to me. Another heartbeat. The woman thrashed in her bonds, which only set the Nevermores at the fence off again.

The men weren't *really* going to do it. They were just trying to scare her—

Vincent flicked his hand up and shouted the word. "Fire!"

Even knowing it was going to happen didn't prepare me for the boom of ten rifles going off at once. The woman's body jerked and jumped, blooms of red spreading from her legs to her forehead.

I swallowed hard. A sudden spurt of nausea made my knees weak, and I slid down the wall with my head against it. Was that how they made room for the new people? Had that woman actually attacked someone? I'd heard the men talking about a woman earlier. Talking about her going crazy. Was that her?

Bile rose at the thought that my presence and the need for a room for me had caused the woman's death. I had to get out of here. This was worse than we'd ever had it at the farm. But, I had Scout, now, and surely I could use him, if he didn't try to attack me, that was. I backed away from the window and lay down on the cot, my hand over the small bump on my belly. Missy sat beside me and laid her head on my belly. I rubbed her ears. "Missy, we've got to get out of here." I had to find a way to protect myself, Sebastian, and our child.

"Think, girl, you're smarter than a bunch of noo-dle-headed army brats." I considered all the possibil-ities, scenarios that could be, might be, and would never be. If I broke out of this place, I'd still have to find a way into the bunker to get Sebastian. Then we'd have to get out of the bunker and over the fence and through the Nevermores. Maybe with the big truck, we could do it. Our chance of success would be even higher with someone helping from the inside.

This was no action movie and I was no MacGyver. I needed more than a paperclip and a gum wrapper to get out of this.

I stood and paced the small room. The air was warm and musty despite the perpetually open win-dow, and the different scents tickled my nose and made me sneeze. Rubbing my face, I looked down at my clothes. I was covered in Sebastian's blood. He was injured and I had no way of knowing if they were tak-ing care of him. Or hurting him further. He healed fast, but that didn't mean they couldn't make it worse.

I swallowed back the fear. Being afraid wouldn't help me. I had to take control. I had to make a plan.

There had to be a way for me to get into the bunker and close to Sebastian. From there, we could find our way out. I had to believe the lies I was telling myself, if for nothing else but to keep me from curling into a mess and crying until Vincent decided what to do with me.

Missy gave a low growl and her ears flipped back. She stood and padded to the door.

A knock startled me even with Missy's warning. My heart picked up speed and adrenaline suddenly surged through me. This could be my chance.

"Mara, it's Sergeant Green. I have water and a couple pieces of bread for you."

My mouth ached at the thought of carby, starchy, white, fluffy bread. "Come in," I said as though I had a choice in what was going to happen. I grabbed Missy around the collar and held her back. I had no illusions about what she thought of these men. They weren't on our side and she knew it.

I backed up a few steps as Green came in, ducking his head and blushing a little. I had an idea, a light bulb moment that might give me a way out of here. If I could manage it.

Seduction was not something that came easily to me. It never had. During our courtship, Sebastian pursued me, not the other way around. Who was I kidding? I was pregnant, at least ten years older than Green, and to be honest, deception wasn't something I was any better at than seduction. I took a deep breath and decided the best thing I could do was be his friend and hope I could inspire some pity or compassion.

"Thank you, Green. I'm sorry I snapped at you earlier. Nero, that's the dog Vincent threw to the Nevermores . . . he was such a sweetie and so well behaved. He wouldn't have been a pain at all." I let my emotions color my words to the point where I truly choked up at the thought of Nero being torn apart.

Green nodded and handed me two slices of brown, stale bread and a large tumbler of water. "I know. My family raised yellow Labs when I was a kid. They were always good dogs, never had a moment's problem out of them long. Vincent can be a real bastard."

I bit into the slightly stale bread and let out a low groan; it wasn't white and fluffy, but it was still damn good. Around my mouthful, I said, "This is amazing. I haven't had bread in so long."

He nodded and went to leave.

"Wait." I swallowed the bite. "Please, I haven't spoken to anyone and I just want to know what's going on out there. Is there any news? Has there been any mention of a cure? Is there anyone trying to help the survivors?"

Green shook his head and folded his arms. "I don't know that I can say anything about anything. As for the outside, the world has pretty much shut down from what we all can tell. There have been transmissions here and there, but nothing for a while now. I think everyone is pretty much on their own."

I took a sip of the water, my mouth dry and my throat tight with the thought that he was telling me the truth. "Is there nowhere safe? I remember a bit on the TV telling people to go somewhere, but it cut off before we actually heard what they said."

He rubbed at his nose and shrugged. "Rumors and gossip float around here lots, but far as we can tell, it's all false information. Nobody really knows what's going on."

"You aren't even really in the army, are you?" I said, remembering the final announcement to come across on the TV warning survivors to steer clear of men claiming government titles and armies.

Green unfolded his arms and swallowed hard. "I would have been, but never got the chance. I didn't . . . they saved me from my brother. He took the shot." His eyes got distant, as though seeing the past.

I gave Missy a piece of the bread. "These people, this Vincent, they aren't really helping others, are they?"

He looked over his shoulder and stepped close to me, completely invading my personal space and making me fight to stand still. Bending close, he whispered in my ear, "I know you don't want to be here, but there's no way out and they have some places bugged, they are using everything they can that runs on batteries. I . . . I'll try and help you. You remind me of my mom." He stepped back, the color on his cheeks high and his eyes bright.

"Thank you," I mouthed and gave him a smile. He smiled back and again started to leave. For a second time, I stopped him. "Wait, how long are they going to keep me and Missy out here? There isn't even a bucket to pee in." The baby was starting to make its presence known to me on a regular basis in the form of potty trips.

Green reached outside the door and pushed a small ice cream pail into the room, shame filling his eyes. "Sorry, but you're going to be here a while. There is nothing I can do about it. When Vincent changes his mind, you'll be brought into the bunker. Until then, you're stuck out here. Sorry."

I knew he couldn't supersede those orders, not without repercussions. The image of the soldier being ripped out of the back of the truck flashed in my mind. None of his friends had even tried to help him. Obviously, this was an army that wasn't all for one and one for all.

I held up my index finger. "Will you do one thing for me?"

His eyes darted from me to the bunker and back again. "I can't promise anything."

I didn't think I was going to get a better offer. "Okay, just tell Sebastian I'm all right. That we'll get out of here together."

Green stared at me as if I'd lost my mind. "I'll try, but I don't think it's a good idea to lie, even to a monster. He . . . "

My breath caught in my throat as I waited for him to finish his sentence. I finally gave up. "He what?"

The kid shook his head. "Nothing."

Only it wasn't nothing. I could see there was more he wanted to say, but fear kept his mouth shut. "It's okay. I do understand." I smiled, even though inside

I wanted to smack him for calling Sebastian a monster. "Just tell him that we'll get out of here together. That's all I ask, even if you don't think he would understand."

He blew out a big sigh. "Sure, if I'm set to watch him, I'll tell him."

The door closed behind Green and I watched the lanky young man walk back to the bunker. His head was low and his shoulders drooped. I noticed he didn't look toward the post where the woman had been shot. She hung there still, and I could easily imagine the sound of flies circling her body. I wished I'd asked him about her. Why in the world would they have shot her? What had she done that had been so bad in this world where so few humans survived? Next time he came, I'd ask him and see if his answer gave me any clues to the men who lived here.

I gripped the window bars and swallowed hard. I let out a low whistle and within a few moments gaunt fingertips slid up the edge of the window. Yellow veins throbbed on the back of Scout's hand. I ripped my second piece of bread in half and pushed it into his fingers. We were trapped, but that didn't mean we were out of options. I gave the other half of the bread to Missy. She took it and gulped it down in one snap of her teeth. Absently, I patted her head, but my eyes were on the Nevermore in front of me.

"Our backs are to the wall now, Scout. But if they think I'm going to just give up, then they've got a shock coming."

Scout chuckled and tapped the bars with his

fingers, then tapped his forehead before slinking away to hide once more. I shook my head and lay down on my cot. It was a bad day when I considered Scout to be my confidant and only other ally I had with me besides a yellow Labrador retriever.

I curled up on my side and Missy rested her head on my knee. Her dark brown eyes said it all.

There was nothing to do now but wait.

CHAPTER EIGHT

Sebastian

"Wake up."

The voice snapped me out of a dead sleep so fast and hard, I lurched to my feet before my brain came fully awake. I stood, my legs shaking and my body unsure of whether it should fight or run.

Images rolled over me as the other Nevermores in the cells around me filled me in on the man in front of me.

He hurts us. Lots of pain. He likes it. Likes to see us bleed.

Uses ropes to hold us down.

Doesn't feed us.

Cages us.

Pain.

That I saw over and over again. The wounds he'd inflicted on the Nevermores he'd caught. I understood that I along with the others were animals that killed, predators, we killed. We didn't torture. We didn't look for ways to draw it out. I blinked my eyes several times. From the shadows of my cell, I could clearly see the man in front of me.

His hair was white and black and his eyes were hard and mean. Angry. I held still, waiting to see what he wanted.

"Get over here, monster. The kid says you can talk. That you can converse."

I didn't move. I held the high ground; no need to give him a leg up.

He pulled a baton from his belt and slammed it against the bars of the cell. The rattling blow echoed off the concrete walls and floor. The other Nevermores gibbered with fear.

He smiled, and it reminded me of something from my past. Was it a man I'd known? That dark, murderous smile. "Either you will talk, or I will make you talk. Honestly, I'd prefer that I get the chance to make you talk. That is much more enjoyable."

I backed a step. The shadows of the cell engulfed me and I knew there was no way his weak eyes could penetrate them.

"Excellent. I think I will enjoy breaking you." He tapped his baton again on the cell, softer this time, almost like an afterthought. I shook my head. Break me?

I didn't have long to think about it.

Two new men came to the cell door. One of them was the kid who'd spoken to me earlier. His face was taut with fear, and he reeked of desperation. In his hands he held a small gun with a dart sticking out of it. Before I could dodge, he'd pulled the trigger and the dart shot forward. I caught it with my hand a split second before it touched the skin of my bare belly.

The other man took a step back. "Shit. Shoot it again, kid!"

"I'm working on it." The kid fumbled with a second dart, got it into the gun and pulled the trigger again.

I stepped to the side and the dart hit the wall behind me. The two men took off running.

Laughter followed them. Not my own, but the other Nevermores.

I rolled the dart in my hand. What was I going to do with it? I bent at the knees and stared at the wall. The concrete had flaked away in this section. Without much effort I was able to place the dart in the hollow. Saving it. For what, I didn't know.

My inattention cost me. A sharp sting in my right hip sent a bolt of panic through me. I grabbed the dart that had buried into my flesh and ripped it out. I held it up, but it was too late. The vial was empty.

I shook my head as the cell spun and swam in front of me. The man who held the dart gun was no longer the kid, but an older male whose eyes were almost as cold as the first man's.

"Boys, get ready. Soon as his knees buckle, we'll head in."

Stupid, stupid man to think I didn't understand him. A snarl fell from my lips and I let my legs buckle at the knees. I fell forward, just barely catching myself on my hands. I was sliding into the abyss of whatever the drug they'd given me was, but I wasn't there yet. The door creaked open and three men stepped inside with ropes at the ready.

"Easy, boys, easy."

The first one reached me and I spun and grabbed his leg. Twisting it hard, I yanked him off his feet and he went down screaming. I whipped around and grabbed the dart I'd only just put in the hollow of the wall. With the feathered needle clenched tightly in my hand, I jammed it into the second man's thigh. He grunted and fell forward on his face in seconds. A distant part of my brain noted that the time it took him to fall, and the time I was taking to go down under the same sedative, was significantly different.

The third man, the one with the gun, stepped out and slammed the door shut. His eyes never left me. They weren't filled with fear as the others were, but fascination. "How much do you understand?"

I glared at him as my vision faded, narrowing with each blink of my eyes. The Nevermores around me flooded my mind with images of food, of . . .feasting.

My belly rolled as the smell of the two men in the cell hit my nose. Flesh, bone, meat, food; it called to me still, whispering that it would fill my belly. That the hunger would abate. They were prey.

I was a predator.

I clenched my hands and teeth along with every other muscle I could in order to hold back the temptation to bury my teeth into their bellies. To tear through to the sweet warm blood and viscera inside and let it slide down my throat. I groaned, the image firing through me, every nerve ending I had wound to the point that I felt as though I would shatter if I so much as looked at them.

I only had to hold on a little longer.

The sedative flowed through my system, helping me hold back the raging hunger, the desires I'd thought I'd buried deeply and walked away from. I couldn't fight the powerful sedative, and slowly it softened both my body and urges. The drug lowered me to the floor until my face was pressed against the cold concrete. My breathing slowed, and my eyes closed. Not quite unconscious, I held the full effects of the sedation at bay. How, I'm not sure. I only know that my heart pounded wildly, and the blood in my veins raced.

Burn it off. That was the thought that filtered through me. I wasn't sure if it was mine, or one of the other Nevermores'. With my eyes closed, the images I saw were that of a wildfire devouring diseased trees in a huge forest. The fire raged and the trees fell. My blood sang hot, burning the sedative the same way the forest was decimated. Slowly, the sedative receded.

"You think he's down this time?"

"Yeah."

Hands gripped my upper arms, dragged me forward. My head lolled and a low growl slipped from me before I could catch it.

"Shit, hurry, man."

Their footsteps picked up their pace, the slap of

hard-bottomed soles on concrete echoing around us. I blew out a sharp breath, fighting to wake myself.

"Here. Put him here."

I was flipped onto my back and hoisted onto a cold slab of steel.

"Heavy bastard."

"That's why they don't float."

I struggled to follow what they were talking about, even though the sedative was almost free of my body. I blinked, my eyes watering with the sudden bright light over my head. I turned my face to the side.

The two males were breathing hard, hands on their knees as they bent at the waist watching me. I made a move to sit up but hit the end of my restraints hard. Both hands, both feet, and my waist were pinned to the table below me. My eyes watered with the high-powered light in the room.

The man on the left, the one with the hard eyes, stood and blew out a breath. "Waste of energy, if you ask me. Vincent isn't a doctor. We should be taking all these specimens to the lab, not doing . . . whatever he is doing up here."

The second man grunted. "I'm just glad to have food and a place safe from these things, Clark."

Clark glanced at him and then looked to me. "You think it's safe to have a cell block full of Nevermores that are somewhat impervious to sedative and mean as a pissed-off hive of wasps?"

I pulled at my restraints again, feeling the one on my left hand—on the far side from the two men—give a little. They chattered back and forth, oblivious to what I was doing.

"Vincent is driven by obsession," Clark said.

The door pushed open and the man with the baton stepped in. "Glad to hear you speak your thoughts, Clark."

The two men squared off, two Alphas in their own right. The tension rose and I pulled on the restraints, the metal giving bit by bit.

"I have never been anything but honest with you, Vincent. It's a fool's errand you're on. You can't save her. Even if this one here," he swept a hand at me, "proves that people can come back, she is gone. Her mind is gone. She was one of the first. There is no way that—"

"Enough!" Vincent roared. "Get out. Both of you."

I was impressed that Clark didn't back down. "You should be taking him to the lab. Let the doctor do what he's good at. Let him find the answers, if there are any—"

Vincent closed the distance between him and Clark, so their faces touched. "I said *enough*. Now get out before I strap you on the table next to him and see which one of you screams first."

Clark still didn't back down, not right away. The lines of his jaw tightened as he flexed and tensed and the way he looked at Vincent said it all. It was a battle that had nothing to do with Nevermores.

But for who ran this place of men and monsters.

That boded well for Mara and me.

Clark and the other male left, the door slamming closed behind them with a thunderous crash. Vincent turned to me.

"Now. You can talk. That boy said you can, and you are most certainly not like the other Nevermores. You protected your wife after you were turned, didn't you?"

I didn't move, didn't take my eyes from him for a second. Neither did I answer him. Alphas like him were never satisfied. No matter what I said or did, he would want more, more, more. Until there was nothing left of me but a shattered shell. If I gave him nothing, there would be pain. Punishment.

I drew a deep breath and settled against the table.

Vincent smiled. "I'm so glad you decided to do this the hard way."

He went to a desk at the foot of the table I was tied to. I blinked a few times, unable to identify what he had in his hands right away. My brain picked through my past memories and the word slid through to me.

Cauterizing gun.

"I think, even if you beg, I won't stop right away. You've irritated me, *Bastian*."

My name on his lips brought a snarl to my own.

He bent and plugged the gun into the wall. "The men don't think that the interrogations are worth the use of power, seeing as they produce so little information." He ran the tip of the gun along the underside of my left foot.

I jerked against the bonds, involuntarily, as my

skin charred instantly under the innocuous tool. I bared my teeth, but kept the scream back. I needed him to come closer to my hand that was almost free before I made my move.

Which meant I had to suffer through whatever he had in mind until he was close enough for me to grab him.

His voice blurred in my ears as he used the gun on my legs, and made his way up my hip. The smell of my flesh burning made my stomach rumble with hunger. Vincent laughed, pausing at my thigh. "Hungry? I could cut a piece of the cooked bits off and feed it to you."

Horror and intense need flicked through me. I closed my eyes. He was looking for a response. I refused to give it to him.

The sound of a knife coming clear of its sheath, then being sharpened on a whetstone set my heart racing. He was going to do it.

"What would you like? Dark meat, or light?"

The door clicked open and he froze. I turned my head to see the kid, Green, standing there. His eyes were wide and his face pale.

"Nevermores are making a push for the eastern fence. Clark said to get you."

"Damn it," Vincent snarled and dropped his knife on the desk. Three quick strides and he was out of the room.

Green remained, though, and I watched him closely. His throat bobbed as he swallowed. "You can understand me, right?"

For him, I would answer. "Yes."

"Mara . . . she asked me to help you. If I untie you, will you go back to your cell?"

Without hurting him. That was what he really wanted to know.

I nodded, knowing it was my only chance out of the torture room. "Yes."

He ran to my side and unstrapped my feet first. A shudder rippled through him as he took in the burn mark. "Shit, he is sadistic."

When he came to my wrists, he paused and his eyes flicked up to me. "Okay, I'm trusting you."

"Why?" The question popped out of me. He swallowed again as if trying to get a loaf of bread down his throat sideways.

"Because even I can see you're different. You . . . you need to be with the doc. He can help everyone if he has you."

Everyone. He released my hands and stepped back. I slid from the table, but the wounds on my feet sent me to my knees. The kid backed away and I followed slowly, crawling.

"Hurry, we have to hurry."

I did as he asked and picked up my speed, following him back to the dark cell. Inside was a bucket of water and half a loaf of bread and a single blanket. I barely got through the door before he slammed it shut.

I made my way to the back of the cage and slumped. My body would heal, I knew that. But the kid, what would happen to him?

Arguing voices floated through the cell block. Green gripped the cell door until his knuckles were white.

"What the actual fuck is going on here?" Vincent roared.

"We had a break in the fence. I thought you were needed," Clark said. They came to stop in front of my cell door. They peered into the darkness, but I doubted they could see me with their human eyes.

Vincent turned to the kid. "How did you get him back into the cell by yourself?"

"He . . . he was hungry so I held the food out and he followed me, and then I threw it in the cell."

"Why?" Vincent didn't yell, didn't scream. His question was all the deadlier for the softness with which it was delivered.

Green dropped his head. "I thought it was going to be a long time fighting off the Nevermores. I thought . . . I thought I was helping."

"Goddamn it!" Vincent slapped his hands on the cell. "He's too smart to let us dart him a second time. What the hell are we going to do now?"

Neither of the other men answered him. In fact, he answered his own question. "Never mind. I have a plan."

He spun and strode away, his boots clicking on the cement.

Clark waited until the upper door slammed and then glanced at Green. "I didn't ask you to move him."

"I know. But . . . he isn't like the others. Mara is right."

He clapped a hand on the kid's shoulder. "Don't take risks like that, Green. It will get you killed. He might seem safe, but he's still a Nevermore."

Green nodded and then turned to leave, pausing out of my sight. "Am I going to be punished?"

Clark shook his head. "Not by me. Vincent might give you latrine duty, though."

The kid should not be killed for helping me. Staying where I was, I smacked my hand against the wall to get their attention. They both looked into the shadows.

"Keep him safe." I rumbled.

Clark jumped, his eyes widened and he seemed to struggle to breathe for a moment. "Green will be safe. I'll make sure of it."

I nodded and slid back into the shadows. Clark stayed a little longer. "I'm going to try and keep you alive, Sebastian. I don't know if you can help the doc change things or not. But you're the only hope we've got."

His footsteps receded and the sound of the upper door being locked echoed through the cells. There was no chatter from the other Nevermores, no images flickering through me. I ate my bread, then curled under the blanket. I wasn't cold so much as I didn't want to turn down a gift from an unexpected ally.

CHAPTER NINE

Mara

The first night I spent in my shack inside the army compound was uncomfortable, to say the least. The tiny space heated through the afternoon, and the breeze that countered the worst of it had fallen silent as the sun disappeared.

I paced as best I could, racking my brain for any answer to how I was going to get Bastian, Missy, and me out of this mess.

Missy watched me for the first bit, but she finally gave up and crawled under the cot to sleep. Even though I was tired, I didn't want to lie down. If an opportunity came when I was lying down, what good was I then?

The creak of a metal door brought my head around. I grabbed the bars in the window and stared into the starlit darkness. Soft footsteps and then a face popped into view.

I bit back a scream as Green stared in at me. Oh shit, Scout was out there in the darkness. I wrapped my fingers around Green's.

"You have to go back inside."

"I brought you food." He shifted a package wrapped in a thin material through the bars to me. Next came a bottle of water. "It's the best I can do."

The soft scrape of fingernails on the back of my shed sent my heart into overdrive. Scout. It had to be.

My words tumbled over themselves with my effort to get them out fast. "Thank you. Now go. You have to go back inside."

He frowned at me. "Vincent is—"

"Green. Go." I flicked my hands at him. The scrape of the nails had subsided, but that didn't mean Scout wasn't there.

Nor did it mean he'd stopped moving.

Green took a half step back, then shook his head. "I'm trying to help you."

"And I'm trying to keep you safe!" I bit the words out. Seeing a kid not much older than Jessica when she turned, knowing he was within feet of a Nevermore.

He took another step and a blur shot out from the side of the shed. Scout tackled Green. They went down in a heap of limbs and snarls. Oh God.

"Scout! Stop!" I dangled the food out the small window. "Stop it, right now. I have food here!"

Scout jerked his head up and stared back at me. "Now, Scout."

His shoulders slumped and he scuttled forward. I dropped the package and he snatched it and ran around the back of the shed. Green pushed to his feet.

"Are you okay?"

"Jesus, Mary and Joseph, you can control them?" He was going backward, his eyes glued on the shed.

"Just go. And please . . . don't tell anyone about him. He listens to me and he could help me get out of here."

Green turned and ran before I could say anything else. I watched him until he made it all the way back to the bunker entrance and let himself in.

I slumped where I was, and put my head on the edge of the window. What could possibly go wrong now?

As if on cue, Scout slid forward around the side of the shed. He looked at up me and then pointed out into the field. I frowned. "What?"

Staying low, he ran across the open section . . . right to the spot where the woman still hung from her bindings. Oh no.

"No, no!"

I'm not sure if he didn't hear me or just ignored me. The body jerked as he did something and then he was running back to me.

A hand held up a hunk of flesh under my window. The smell was . . . meat left out too long in the sun, on the verge of rot. I gagged and stumbled back. "No, you eat it."

He grunted and hefted it up a bit higher.

"Scout, go!"

The smell had completely invaded the small space and my stomach couldn't handle it. I dropped to my knees and heaved in the corner until my belly was empty of what little food and water I had.

Water. At least I still had that. I took a small drink from the water bottle, swished it through my mouth and spit. Then another drink to replace the liquid I'd lost.

Fatigue hit me hard. The loss of adrenaline, the fear, the sudden vomit session. That was enough. I slid onto the cot and balled the thin blanket under my head to act as a pillow. Missy crawled out from under the bed and got onto the cot with me. I laughed as she wormed her way around, finally settling in Nero's usual spot against my belly. Too hot by far, I didn't care. I dropped an arm over her and she tucked her head onto my shoulder so her nose was right in my ear. Her soft breathing lulled me to sleep and I fell into a dream I couldn't wake from, no matter how hard I tried.

Images flickered. Of eating the woman's flesh. Of sneaking back for more. The taste of her blood on my lips, licking my fingers clean. I looked back at the shed, only I was looking through another's eyes.

Alpha's mate is trapped. How do I help her?

Those images faded and others flowed to me, as if I stood in a river and the water around my legs was thoughts.

I looked through the fence around the barracks, but from the outside looking in. I ran my hands over the smooth metal and could almost feel the way it rubbed against my palm. Sensation was coming back. My fingers came together one at a time. I glanced over my shoulder and a Nevermore approached me. My mate, a big male that had no hair on the top of his head or chest. He dropped his mouth to my shoulder and leaned into me.

Soon we will get in. The two-legged deer will make a mistake and we will have them. Free our packs.

Fill our bellies.

What of the one in the shed? She is . . . almost like us. Her thoughts run, though, like rain through the trees. I cannot follow them.

That jerked me awake.

I lay on the small cot, my heart out of control, beating as though it would try to free itself from my chest. Panic set my adrenaline coursing hot in my veins.

"Just a dream, Mara. It was just a dream." Only I whispered the words because nothing about what I'd seen felt like a dream at all. Nothing about it made me think that what I'd seen had been my mind playing tricks on me.

I slid off the end of the cot and Missy rolled into the hollow where my body had been. She gave a soft snort but didn't wake. I went to the window and stared out at the spot where the woman's body was.

Scout was crouched beside her.

On the other side of the fence were two

Nevermores. A male and a female, his mouth on her shoulder.

And they were looking straight at me.

CHAPTER TEN

Sebastian

The burn wounds healed by the next morning. Vincent didn't come back. Green brought food.

He put a bundle of food on the floor and whispered, "Sedative is in it."

As much as the hunger bit at my belly, I stayed put in the darkness. Green left the food and went to the other Nevermores, feeding them as well. Several lunged for him.

Leave him, I sent to them. They startled, but I sent them the image of staying clear of the cell while Green was there again. *He will help us.*

Doubt flickered back, but none of them were as strong as me. So they listened.

Green came back to stand in front of my cell. "They've never been so quiet. You did something, didn't you?"

I nodded. "Yes."

A smile twitched his lips. "Thanks. I'm . . . I'm glad I'm helping you and Mara."

At her name I stepped forward. I couldn't find the words, couldn't form the question on my clumsy lips.

He bobbed his head. "She's safe. But," he leaned closer, "I took food to her and a Nevermore jumped me. She called him Scout. She stopped him from eating me."

I nodded, relief flowing through me. Knowing Scout was out there trying to protect Mara eased some of the fear I had. What if Vincent decided to try and torture her? She was pregnant and would lose the baby for sure.

Maybe I could reach Scout with mind speak? I wasn't sure this far apart I could, but I would try.

"Thank you." I managed to get the words out.

Green grinned and gave me a hand signal with one thumb up. I knew it meant something good, but I couldn't mimic it. My hands wouldn't comply.

The kid walked away and a sudden urge flowed through me, pushed on me by the Nevermores from outside the walls.

I wrestled with the urges they pushed as a unit. Any single Alpha couldn't have broken through my barriers like this, but as a pack . . .

Hunger and anger and frustration tangled up inside me, not even my own. I grabbed the plate of food between my two hands and flung it on the opposite wall. A roar escaped me, one that was picked up by the other Nevermores until the sound bounced and echoed inside my head over and over. A cacophony of caged frustration.

Of the need to move and run and be free of this.

My body shook as I snapped my mouth shut on the sound and I dropped to a crouch. My mind fuzzed over and I struggled to remember why I didn't grab the two-legged deer. Was that my thought? I wasn't sure. I tried to block out the other Nevermores but they were in my head now and they wouldn't let go.

Thoughts of chasing the two-legged deer, of scattering them, hamstringing them, of tasting their blood. A groan slipped out of me with the thought of warm, sweet flesh on my tongue. I wanted . . . to be free of what was left of my past.

I shook my head, grabbed at my hair, and struggled to hold onto what was left of me. The two worlds that belonged to me, the one of human and the one of Nevermore collided inside my head and I could not pull them apart. They tangled like snakes writhing around one another, shooting pain through my head. I dropped to my knees, a high-pitched keening slipping from my lips. What was happening? Who was I? What was I?

Mara. Jessica. The pack. Running free. Caged. Fighting. Blood. Desire. Lust. Love.

The images from the other Nevermores battered at me, flooding me with *their* desires, filling me with what they believed. That we were one and that as a pack we would survive. To leave behind my past, to let it go as they had and embrace the creature I was now.

I could not deny it.

One last effort, one last breath as I struggled to swim through the confusion of my mind. My name, what was my name? Bastian? No.

Something else. Alpha. I was an Alpha.

Fire . . . I'd left her behind. She was my mate. Wasn't she?

And I had to get back to her . . . and our child.

CHAPTER ELEVEN

Mara

They kept me in the utilitarian barracks for another four days with nothing more than a bucket to pee in. Green continued to bring me food and water rations twice a day, as well as cleaning stuffs for the vomit. I continued to talk to him, building on our tentative friendship. His eyes darted around for Scout, but the Nevermore kept himself scarce in the daylight hours. Thank God.

Green sat outside my shack and spoke quietly while I ate my meagre meal.

"My mother and older sister were all I had left—Dad took off with his secretary a few years ago. Both Mom and Jana took the shot as soon as they had enough money. They thought it would solve their problems."

I swallowed my bite of food. "What kind of problems did they have?"

"My mom gained a lot of weight after Dad cheated on her. She wanted to lose it all and find a new guy, I guess. Jana was terrified of getting sick. She was a hyper something or other."

"Hypochondriac?" I offered.

"Yeah, that." There was a dull tone to his voice that didn't bode well.

"You don't have to say anything else."

"No, I mean. It's good to talk about it, right?"

I wasn't so sure, but I didn't want to dissuade him either. Morbid curiosity had its claws deeply in me. "I'm here. I'll listen."

He sniffed twice. "Jana and Mom, they turned within minutes of each other. Mom attacked me first and I . . ." His words hitched and I reached out the window, put a hand on the top of his head.

"You don't have to," I repeated.

"I killed her. I didn't mean to, but she fell on me and I had a knife and it was over so fast." A sob ripped out of him. He reached up and took my hand. I clung to him and he to me.

"I'm so, so sorry you had to do that. I . . . I had a similar experience with the first Nevermore I killed. I didn't mean to. I didn't want to. But I wanted to live."

He was quiet a moment as he pulled himself together. "I was able to knock Jana out, and then I grabbed some stuff and ran for it. I'm hoping that Bastian . . . that if he can come back, maybe Jana can too."

I squeezed his fingers, my heart hurting for him. "I hope so, too." Only, I wasn't so sure. Sebastian had never fully turned. Not really. There had always been something residual in him that was my husband and not full Nevermore. I didn't want to burst Green's bubble, though.

He cleared his throat. "When I got outside, there were Nevermores everywhere. We lived in a subdivision, you know? They were spilling out of the houses like I'd kicked an anthill."

"How did you get away?"

"Clark came driving down the street and ran the monsters over; I jumped in the back of the truck and we came up here. He said I would be safe. He was right, except for Vincent." He shuffled his feet and removed my hand from his. He stood and faced the window. "I think they're going to take you into the bunker tomorrow."

My eyes widened. This was what I'd been waiting for, the chance to get closer to Sebastian. "Really? Why the sudden change?"

"You know that woman they shot?"

I swallowed hard, dread filling me. So much for hope. "I'm next, aren't I?"

Green shook his head. "No, you aren't like her. Fran tried to kill Vincent in his sleep. He caught her with a big kitchen knife held to his throat. She almost did him in. At least that's what he says."

He didn't sound terribly upset by the whole thing. I frowned and tipped my head. "So you didn't like her, either? Was she that awful?"

Green shrugged. "I didn't really know her. She was kept separate from most of us. She was only for the officers, you know." Then he blushed, his face going red. "I mean . . . I didn't . . ."

I shushed him with a wave of one hand. I knew exactly what he meant and I did not need it spelled out for me. If Vincent thought he was going to use me as some kind of sex slave I might try and kill him too. Can't say I blamed the woman one bit if she'd tried to stop him.

As if reading my thoughts, Green continued.

"I don't know why she would try to kill him. It didn't make sense to me or Clark. Fran and her daughter were taken in, and she said she didn't mind sleeping with the officers." He paused and shook his head. "It's not Vincent's fault Danielle got outside the gates. Ron was on guard that night and fell asleep. We aren't really very good at this."

My head snapped up and my eyes narrowed. "The woman had a daughter?"

Green nodded. "Yeah, she was about ten years old, I guess. I didn't see her much either. She spent most of her time locked in her room." Again Green flushed as if he'd said too much. He changed the subject.

"I think the real reason Vincent is bringing you in is that something's inside the fence here. Something that's been eating Fran's body at night. We don't have enough power to keep a camera system up and running to catch it and they're afraid it might be one of the Nevermores busted in here somehow." His eyes met mine. We both knew full well there was a Nevermore inside the compound. Scout.

"You didn't tell them a Nevermore attacked you? Why?"

He squeezed his eyes shut tightly for a moment. "Because. I think you and Bastian are the key to figuring out how to bring people back from the shot. I want to help you. And you said you could control that Nevermore and you did."

"Thank you," I whispered. Another thought hit me on the heels of the gratitude. "If they suspect it's a Nevermore, why would they keep sending you out as often as they are?"

Green's eyes snapped up to meet mine. I let out a breath with a whoosh of air. "Of course. *That's* why you've been sent out here, to draw it out. You are part of the bait, same as me. That's why they left me in here so long. To see if it would attack me."

Green shook his head, the doubt apparent in his eyes. "No, they wouldn't do that."

"You so sure you'd bet your life on it? They aren't your friends any more than they are mine, Green."

We stared at each other, neither one of us backing down. I knew I was right and the sudden flicker of his eyelids told me he knew it, too. Without another word, he took my empty water glass and left. As so often was the case, his shoulders were slumped and his head down.

I watched him go from the window. "Kid, you are going to get yourself killed if you keep believing in the wrong people."

As soon as he went into the bunker, Scout sidled

up to the window and I handed him half a piece of bread. Missy nudged my hand and gave a soft whine. I dropped the rest of the bread to her. It wasn't much, but it would have to do for all three of us.

"Scout, they're going to take me inside soon. You wait outside, here by the shed when I go in. I'll bring Sebastian out and then we can all go home," I said. I had no idea what we'd do once we got home, but it seemed like the only place to go that might be safe. Or maybe it was just that I knew the dangers there. I knew I could survive on the farm.

Scout grunted around his mouthful of bread, then slipped into the shadows around the back side of the shed. The scratch of his fingernails on the wood didn't bother me. I liked knowing he was there. A secret weapon. I don't know how he kept out of sight. Then again, there had been no movement outside the bunker other than Green bringing me food.

Even the other Nevermore packs had gone quiet. I shuddered thinking about the dream from the other night. Of seeing through their eyes, of feeling the emotions washing through them and how they considered me almost like one of them. But why? Why would they think I was almost a Nevermore? It had to be because of my connection with Sebastian and Scout.

I leaned so I could see more of the fence. Here and there, Nevermores moved in the shadows of the bush and trees on the far side. Faint flickers of a leg, or torso, the glimmer of their strange eyes. Searching for them was like watching for deer as they ghosted through the bush. Deer that had teeth and insatiable hunger for flesh.

I pulled away from the window and sat on the cot. "We can do this, Missy. I don't know how, but we'll do this."

She gave me her trademarked soulful look as though she understood completely. I put a hand on top of her head and gave her love.

The next day came slowly and the heat of the mid-summer rose early, which turned the small room into my own personal sauna. Sweat soaked through my shirt and pants as I lay on my bed, praying Green would come soon with rations. At that moment, though my stomach was empty and growling for food, it was the sweet taste of lukewarm water I craved.

Missy panted softly under the cot, the coolest part of the shed. I was tempted to crawl underneath with her.

Footsteps thumped toward my room and I stood, wobbling a little as the room spun. Weak from lack of food and water as well as the heat, I did my best to stand and face whoever was about to come through the door.

The click of a key in a lock, the second pop of the lock opening, then the door flung wide.

Sunlight streamed through, blinding me for a moment. Vincent peered in and wrinkled his long nose.

"You need a bath and clean clothes if you are to be any help to us. I won't stand for lack of hygiene in my group." He snapped his fingers and Green strode in looking grim. With his back to Vincent, he gave me a wink as he grabbed my arm. Missy leapt up and moved to my side as Green pulled me along with him.

We got ahead of Vincent, and Green whispered to me, "Stick close, I'll look out for you. Clark will, too."

Missy trotted a few steps ahead, her tail and ears up and her head swivelling from side to side as she kept her eyes on everything she could. The Nevermores on the fence rattled the line and she gave a low growl, but didn't move toward them.

I gave Green a small smile. "Thanks." He was nothing more than a tall boy, barely out of childhood, but he was trying to protect me. I had a feeling it would more likely be me looking out for him when it came down to the crunch, but that was okay. Stepping quickly, we reached the bunker in less than a minute. I glanced back at Vincent, who dawdled behind us. He was crouched low over something in the dirt. Maybe a footprint of Scout's? What else could have caught his attention so fully?

Movement at the edge of the wooden shed I'd been in caught my gaze. Scout crept forward and made eye contact with me, then pointed at Vincent. We might not have another chance, but I wasn't sure it would help us to kill the leader of the men here. What if he wasn't as bad as Green thought? What if I could get him to let us go? There was no guarantee no matter what I decided.

I took a shallow breath. Like a gun resting in my hands, Scout was a weapon waiting on my order. Vincent's death, if I told Scout to kill him, would be on my shoulders. No different than the raiders that had broken into our home in Fanny Bay.

I closed my eyes and shook my head. Scout paused and stared at me, then began to creep forward, ignoring my command.

"No!" I twisted out of Green's hands, and ran toward Vincent. Missy shot forward, putting herself between Scout and me.

Vincent's mouth circled into a wide surprised *O,* and he didn't even try to grab me as I rushed past him and put myself between him and Scout. It wasn't that I cared if Vincent lived or died, not really; it was the fact I needed Scout. If he got himself killed, because he didn't listen to me, it was one less ally for me to count on. And I needed all the help I could get.

As I drew close to Scout, he started to growl. I didn't stop. Instead I squared my shoulders and increased my speed, stopping only when my toes were less than a foot from his. Missy was to my right, her body hunched low to the ground and her hackles raised. But she seemed to understand that while Scout was a Nevermore, he wasn't like the others. He was on our side.

Kind of.

I pointed at the shack behind him. "Scout, go. Go back to the shed."

He stared at me with his lips curled back over his teeth. He shook his head once, touched his chest and then pointed at me. Another time maybe I would have thought it was great he was so bonded to me. Maybe.

I frowned down at him and clapped my hands with a sharp report. "Now!" Missy barked once as if to emphasize my words and instructions.

He flinched, and I pointed again to the shed with a jerk of my arm. He grumbled and scratched at his crotch before backing away with his head down. He glanced at me like a surly child being sent to his room. But he went and that was all that mattered.

"I have never seen any of them respond to someone like that. How did you train him?" Vincent asked, the awe in his voice not making me feel any better about what I'd just done.

"I don't know." I had an idea about why Scout listened, but I wasn't about to share it with Vincent. A part of me wished I'd let Scout attack him. I glanced at Vincent, noting the two handguns he had, one on either side of his hips.

If I'd let Scout take him down, I had no doubt that the Nevermore would have been killed.

Vincent was not someone to be trusted, I knew that already, even if Green hadn't filled me in on some of the things he'd done.

When it came to Scout, though, I wasn't giving my secrets away. I'd seen how the pack worked and how they revered the Alpha's mate. I'd seen it even in the Nevermores here that surrounded the barracks. Scout knew I belonged to Sebastian, better than any other Nevermore did. In a strange way, I'd become a member of the pack, a member that was in higher standing than Scout as a lowly member. Which meant I could push him around, just as a true Alpha's mate would. From his reaction, I wasn't far off the mark in my theory. I didn't want to believe the dream I'd had of my connection to the Nevermores meant anything. But even I could see it did.

Green grabbed my arm from behind, apologizing to Vincent, "I'm sorry, I wasn't holding her tight enough."

"It's quite all right, Green," Vincent said. "In fact, I think you've done us a service by letting her go. By allowing me to see just what she's capable of. Perhaps torture isn't the best way to tame the beasts. I think perhaps we can finally begin to make real progress with the monsters. A beauty is perhaps what we need to make the monsters behave, yes?"

He stared at me, a slow smile spreading across his angular face, bright white, perfect teeth flashing at me. I swallowed hard. I didn't want to become a commodity to Vincent or his army in any way, but if I was going to be valuable, at least it was for something I could do other than lie flat on my back.

"Missy, to me." I snapped my fingers and she heeled to my side in a flash. Though more than once she looked over her shoulder.

They hustled us into the cool of the bunker, and the door slammed shut, the sound of the lock sliding into place loud and echoing. Stepping down into the underground safe house, I let out a sigh of relief even though it was too dark to see after the bright sunlight. The dank air was cool on my skin and a welcome change to the sauna I'd left.

"Green, you have duties. Attend to them." Vincent stepped up and put a hand on my arm, all but pushing Green away. Missy snarled and snapped her teeth at Vincent. He let go and his foot curled back.

"Don't you dare!" I shoved him hard so he bounced against the wall. I didn't think I had it in me, but then again, this was Missy. She was my girl.

Green sucked in a sharp gasp. "Mara, don't."

"No! I won't let him hurt my dog. Not when she's protecting me. She's looked out for me far longer than anyone else." I held my ground, refusing to back down from either man.

Vincent slowly pushed himself off the wall and straightened his clothes. "Take her to my office, Green. And wait with her there."

Green reached out and put a careful hand on my forearm. "Come on."

He hurried me through the halls of flickering lights and cool air. "Try not to piss him off, Mara. He's not worth your life."

"Bullies get off on bullying. I'm not going to let him bully me or Missy."

Green stopped in front of a door that didn't look different than any other. He opened the door and walked in behind me. The room was set up with a desk and a shelf behind it with a few books stacked haphazardly.

Missy sniffed around the room, pushing her nose against several books before continuing on her perusal of the room.

The door opened almost right away and Vincent stepped in. "Green, out."

Green nodded, giving me a look that clearly said to lay low. I arched an eyebrow back at him. No way was I letting Vincent push me around. Not if I could do anything about it.

Vincent shut the door behind Green. He stepped forward so he was right behind me, mere inches between my back and his chest. I didn't move an inch.

"With your help training the monsters, we can finally take over the city from Donavan. I will make him pay for what he's taken from me." Vincent's voice was right in my ear. The heat from his breath made my skin crawl. The smell of garlic and the faint curl of body odor blended together into an unpleasant cologne. He placed his hands on my upper arms. "I like a strong woman. And women are so few and far between, now."

"Don't touch me. I don't care what you think. I am not going to be anything to you. And I'm not helping you make anyone pay." I jerked away from him. Vincent glared at me and I glared back. Missy, as always, put herself between us. I dropped a hand to her, holding her back. Or maybe holding her away from him.

"You *will* help me, Mara." He straightened his shirt, though it didn't need it.

I lifted my chin. "And if I don't?"

"We will both find out just how much pain your big boy can handle. So far, he's only had a taste of what I am capable of."

I choked on what he was saying. "You've tortured him?"

"Pain is the path to knowledge. Of understanding. I am a very good guide, Mara. You'd best remember that. You help me, and I won't hurt you or your pets." He glanced at Missy who snarled at him silently.

Vincent gave me a sharp nod. "I see you understand, finally."

I swallowed hard. Vincent knew my weakness. I steeled my back. That could only mean one thing.

I had to figure out his weakness, too.

CHAPTER TWELVE

Sebastian

The two-footed deer, the same as always, young and nervous, brought me a meal. "This one is clean. You can eat it."

The words floated through me and I wondered at them. Why weren't they images? How could I understand them? Nevermore. Man. Which was I?

The Nevermores around us chattered softly, clicking their tongues and teeth, trying to pull me back to them. I reached for the food and pulled it in. In front of me, the two-footed deer sat against the cage bars. Close enough for me to grab him.

Grab him.

Kill him.

Free us.

I snaked my arm out and around his neck before he could react. With a yank, I clanked his head back and knocked him out against the bars. Or I thought I did.

He struggled against my hold, his fingers digging into my arm. "Mara. You and Mara."

That name shocked me out of the fog in my head. "Mara?"

"Yes, Mara is coming. She's here." His words were partially strangled but I heard them. I understood.

I blinked and let him go as I shook my head. The Nevermores pushed their images at me, doing their best to force me to hear them, to do as they wanted.

I put my hands over my ears and slid back into the darkness away from the front of the cage. I didn't want to hurt the kid. The boy. Not a two-footed deer. He wasn't prey. He was like me. Like Mara.

I just had to hold on long enough to see her. To  touch her and then . . . then what?

I didn't know.

But until I saw her, I would fight whatever was going on inside my head. I would fight it and hope she would help me to understand.

To help me be free.

CHAPTER THIRTEEN

Mara

Vincent hit an intercom button. "Green. Get back here."

"I want to see Sebastian," I said. "I know he's in here and I want to see him. I don't trust you not to have already killed him."

"You will see him when I'm damn good and ready to let you!" Vincent's voice was deadly calm as he made his way around to his desk.

Again he straightened his shirt and began to pace. "First, you will get clean. You stink to the heavens. Then we will discuss the training of the Nevermores that you will be doing, and how I want to see the progress happen. Perhaps if you show your usefulness, I will let you see your precious Sebastian. But not one second before."

There was a tentative rap of knuckles on the door and Green peered in.

His face was a blotchy red and white as though

he'd been running and there was a mark against his throat. Like the beginnings of a bruise.

"Vincent?"

"Take her and get her cleaned up. I can barely breathe with her stench."

I couldn't stop myself. "That's rich coming from one who stinks like BO and garlic."

Vincent flushed red and Green grabbed me quickly, dragging me from the room. Missy leapt after me.

"Why are you antagonizing him?"

"I'm not. I'm standing up for myself. If everyone did, he wouldn't be in charge. I wish I'd let Scout take him."

Green flinched as he turned me to the left and then down a flight of stairs.

"Don't say things like that. You and I both know he would have shot him."

He paused and opened a door on our right. "Missy can wait for you here. This will be your room. The rest of the barracks are filled with the other men. Those that are left, anyway."

I snapped my fingers at Missy and she went into the room, reluctantly. "I won't be long. You wait for me here." I bent and gave her a hug, then rubbed both her velvety ears. I hoped I wasn't lying. That I would be back in the room with her in no time and not fighting off some lecherous old army pervert.

I shook myself. No, it was no good to think like that.

"This way." Green tipped his head. He no longer held onto my arms so I followed closely. Around us were the whispers of men as we passed by their rooms in the semi-darkness of the poorly lit halls. The sounds of the buzzing lights and deep rumble of voices left me feeling as though bugs crawled over my skin.

One more corner and we stood in the doorway of a huge multi-person shower. There were a few sky-lights that let in natural light, glinting off the beige tiles. Shower heads lined both sides of the wall with no curtains anywhere.

"Here, you can get cleaned up and I'll get you fresh clothes. Vincent . . . he's weird about smells and such."

"He stinks, but no one else can?" I asked.

Green gave a nervous laugh and rubbed his throat. "I know. But this is an easy way to keep him happy." He handed me a threadbare towel and a small bar of soap. "I won't be long with the clothes. I'll knock before I come in." He was gone and I stood staring around a moment.

I waited a full minute, then put my hand to the knob and opened the door a crack.

"Is there something you need, ma'am?" a man's voice asked from somewhere in the hall. Someone had been set to watch the door to make sure I didn't leave. Nice.

"No, thank you." My manners came into play de-spite the fact I was a captive of these men. That I'd even warranted a guard on my bathroom time was telling.

I didn't know what was going to happen, or how I was going to handle it. But at that moment, the thought and temptation of hot water overrode any other concerns I had.

I stripped and stepped up to the closest shower-head, then turned it on full blast. Ice cold water hit me in the face and I gasped and choked on it, but forced myself to stay under. So much for the hot water I'd momentarily dreamed about. I scrubbed furiously with the small bar of soap and was able to at least get the layers of dirt and sweat removed from the last few days.

The cold didn't ease and my skin began to hurt. I turned it off, dripping wet with nothing more than the threadbare towel. I scrubbed it over my skin fast, the friction building heat. Reminding me of the shower with Sebastian after the walk in the broom. He'd towelled me dry and we'd made love, laughing and romping together with abandon. That was before Nevermore came into our lives. My eyes pricked with tears and I dashed them away. No, I wouldn't fall to pieces. Sebastian needed me to be strong. Our baby needed me to be strong.

"Mara, are you done?"

"I'm here." The towel barely covered what God gave me and did little to stave off the cold air.

Green stepped into the room and put a pile of clothes on a section of the floor that was dry. The pants were khakis and the top was a simple button-down shirt. Unisex, nothing fancy, but they were clean and I was grateful. He turned around quickly so he didn't see me.

"Here are clothes. I'll just be outside when you're dressed."

I bent and grabbed the clothes. "I'll be quick. I'm freezing."

He hurried out and the door clicked shut again.

Once fully dressed, I opened the door.

Before Green could say anything, I lifted my hand to stall him. "I want to see my husband. Where is he?"

Green shook his head, "He's down with the others. He's okay, but I can't take you to him. Vincent wants to see you right away; I don't want to get caught disobeying him again."

Again? What had he done?

"I'm not going to Vincent until I see Sebastian. I need to know he's alive. We can run. I'll take the blame if we have to, you can say I got away from you."

Green let out a sigh and looked down the hallway. There were no other men, despite the fact I'd had a guard only a few minutes before.

He shook his head and my heart sank.

"Mara," he said, "if we run, you can maybe see him for twenty seconds at best."

My head snapped up and I nodded, my mouth unable to even form a thank you past the shock that he'd actually agreed to my request.

We took off at a fast jog, down three more flights of stairs to what he informed me was the lowest level. The section was split into cells, not unlike a jail, with each cell holding at least one Nevermore. As we hurried past, they reached out. Their eyes roved me, narrowing one by one.

But not a sound escaped them. That was unusual. With the pack at home, if we were ever this close there was at least a growl or two, a snarl of hunger. Something.

"Why are they so quiet?"

Green glanced at me as his feet slowed. "Vincent wants to show how the Nevermores can be trained and so he had us capture a male and a female—at least that was it to start with. He punished them when they did anything he didn't think they should. Like making noise when we walked by. Now they stay quiet. Or they did until Sebastian showed up."

I glanced into a cage as we passed to see a form curled into a tight ball, just visible at the edge of the light from the hall. Burn marks oozed from various parts of the Nevermore's body.

"He tortured them," I said. Once more I wished I'd let Scout attack Vincent. If I had helped him, we could have ended Vincent right then. But I didn't know. I didn't know just how bad Vincent was.

The next cage showed a very pregnant woman, which shocked me. Her wrists and ankles were raw where it was obvious she'd been tied up and struggled against her bonds. Her skin was covered with the faint lines of the broom flower.

"That's Clark's wife. Or ex-wife, I guess. They were separated when she took the shot and already pregnant. Vincent is very curious to see what happens when the baby is born," Green said.

I looked away. "Please, just take me to Sebastian."

"Here," Green stopped in front of the last cage on the block. He stepped to the side to let me pass. "Vincent thinks we can use the Nevermores as a trained army to take over Donavan's—that's the doc—compound. At least, that's what he told us and we believed him. I'm not so sure it's a good idea, though. The doc thinks he can help the Nevermores."

His words were like flies around me. I heard him, but I didn't focus on him at all. I stared into the last cage, its gloomy interior not showing me anyone. "Sebastian?" I called out. A shadow shifted and stood tall. In two strides, he was at the front of the cage. For a moment, his eyes were blank, without recognition. And then his hands reached for me through the bars.

"Wait for me at the other end of the block," I said to Green as I took Sebastian's hands in my own, my eyes never leaving his.

"I'm not supposed to leave you alone, and last time I was here—"

"Green, you gave me twenty seconds, at least let me have those moments alone. Besides, there is nowhere for me to go." I glanced at him and he nodded slowly.

With a cough and a hand to his throat, he shuffled down the way we'd come.

"I'm so sorry, Bastian," I whispered.

He grunted and pulled me up against the bars, our bodies separated only by the cold metal. Sebastian pressed his lips to my forehead, and his hands roved up and down my back before they finally settled on my hips. I pressed a hand against the scar on his shoulder that only days ago had been a bullet hole. There were other wounds, now, especially on his leg. Burn marks like the ones the other Nevermore had.

"Vincent hurt you. I'm going to kill him." The force of my words shocked us both. He grinned down at me.

"Mara."

I smiled at him. "I'm glad you're okay."

He lifted the top of one lip in a half smile, took my hand and slid it down his chest before he pressed my palm against the evidence of his arousal. For the first time in a long time, I blushed, a rush of heat firing my blood. He tipped his head to one side and pressed harder against my hand, his eyes softening with desire. I flexed my hand and he groaned, leaning his head against the bars and grinding his hips into my fingers. I sucked in a deep breath, my body aching to be touched, to feel again his heart beat against my own. Footsteps echoed and we pulled back, both of us trembling and our faces flushed.

There had been no change between us. No matter what he became, I would love him and he loved me. That alone gave me hope.

"Mara, I need to take you to the war room now. Vincent is waiting and he's going to know we took a detour if we put this off any longer. We do not want to piss him off further than you already have," Green said.

"Okay." I touched Sebastian on the back of his hand. "I'll be back soon."

He gave me a slow nod and slid back into the shadows once more. He was alive. He loved me. We would find a way through this. I had to believe it.

I followed Green as we jogged back the way we'd

come, stopping before we reached the floor where the showers were. I did my best to memorize the turns and twists of the tunnels, the stairwells and room numbers—because the minute I got the chance, I was going to bust us out of here.

CHAPTER FOURTEEN

Sebastian

Her touch drove the images of the Nevermores out of my mind and helped me grab hold of myself. I wanted to keep her with me because if she left and I forgot again, what would happen? What if I attacked her the way I'd attacked the kid?

I hung my head in the shadows and waited. She said she would come back. Mara would come back and I would wait for her no matter how long it took.

"Always." I breathed the word and the Nevermores took up a cry that battered against my head. They tried to make me let the images in, to listen to them and the things they wanted me to see. It took all I had to block them, and then I realized Vincent hadn't been bringing just any Nevermore to their compound.

Nearly all those in the cells around me were Alphas of varying degrees. I made myself pick through the images, looking for one that would give him away. This was an attack designed to bring me into line.

The minds that connected with mine were strong, but so far all of them could be pushed away when I concentrated on them. Silencing them one at a time. Sweat slid over my body as I worked at controlling them, stopping them from their coordinated attack on my mind.

But the one I searched for remained hidden. A powerful Alpha, one who knew how to hide. One who was stronger than me.

I slumped into the back corner and tipped my head back. He would find me, or I would find him.

And then we would see who was the stronger. I sent an image to the other Nevermores, one that made more than one of them suck in a sharp gasp.

I stood with a dead male at my feet, my head thrown back as I roared my victory.

"Alpha." I growled the word and the Nevermores didn't answer. Not this time.

CHAPTER FIFTEEN

Mara

The war room was covered in maps of the area and the world in general. A large wooden table dominated the center. The top was polished to a brilliant sheen that reflected the few lights in the room, where there wasn't paper.

Vincent sat at the head of the table. His army fatigues were neat and tidy, and his face unreadable. To the left of him stood a man I hadn't seen since the day we were taken from the farm. Clark, who I assumed was Vincent's second-in-command. He had his hands tucked behind his back and he didn't even look at me. Just stared straight ahead.

"It took you long enough." Vincent stood and leaned on the table.

I shrugged and tried not to let my exertion from the run show. "I wanted to get clean. As you pointed out, I was filthy, and if you want perfection, you can't get it done in thirty seconds."

"Don't sass him," Green whispered.

Vincent rolled his shoulders, stood upright, and clasped his hands behind his back just like Clark.

"What I want from you, Mara, is simple. You are going to help me train the Nevermores. If you don't, I will kill your . . . Sebastian. If you still flout my authority, you will find yourself in an unfortunate situation where you will no longer be carrying your child. And if you continue to fight me—I will kill you. It is really that straightforward."

The blood fled from my face and pooled somewhere in the bottom of my legs. I swayed, but managed to stay standing.

He couldn't be serious, could he? Was Vincent so cold as to cause me to miscarry if I upset him? I stared into his pale gray eyes, searching for a spark of compassion, something that would tell me he was exaggerating. I found nothing but a smirk of satisfaction. He knew he had me.

He spun on one heel and tapped on the chalkboard behind him. "Perhaps this will help you see reason as to why I would hold you to such high standards."

I stared, not sure if what I was seeing was correct or not. There were six words written in perfect capital letters. I read them out loud. "CONTROL OF CURE, CONTROL OF POWER."

My mouth dropped open and I took an involuntary step forward. My heart pounded with a sudden and unspoken hope. "There's a cure for Nevermore?"

He smiled, but it was no warmer than the look in his eyes.

"I thought perhaps that might get your attention. You will see that I can be fair to those who are loyal to me, to those who are obedient to me." He paused and nodded as if to himself. "If you help me take Donavan's compound by way of the Nevermores, I will give to you and your Sebastian whatever cure Donavan has cooked up."

I looked at Clark, thinking of his wife in the cells below. "If there is a cure, why aren't they using it?"

Clark didn't answer me.

Vincent snorted. "The cure is in Donavan's compound on the harborfront of the city. It's where he and his scientists have been working on it night and day. They've produced some phenomenal effects already." He gave me a tight-lipped smile. "We are starting to see the realities of what Nevermore first promised. Men with strength and immunity to disease. Men who heal a bullet wound in days. Men who can be warriors."

My legs started to tremble and I slowly lowered myself into my chair, not wanting to show weakness. Vincent wanted an army of Nevermores. An army of monsters to take out this Donavan—Doc, as Green called him. But to me, it sounded like Donavan was the good guy.

The door opened and I turned to see Green bringing in a tray of steaming food. I sniffed and my saliva glands seemed to explode in my mouth. Chicken noodle soup and garlic toast. My stomach growled voraciously and I had to swallow several times to keep myself from drooling.

"Eat. I can't have you falling down while you train the Nevermores. Don't worry, it's safe to eat. I can't afford to waste you."

"Safe?" It took me a moment to understand that he meant it wasn't drugged or poisoned.

He pulled the bowl of soup close to him, lifted the spoon and took a slurp. "Safe." He pushed it slowly back to me.

A part of me wanted to refuse him, but he'd already made it clear that Sebastian's life was on the line, and he had taken some himself. I sipped at the soup, then slurped back a spoonful of noodles, the cheap yellow broth as delicious as a gourmet meal. The slightly stale garlic bread crunched and I fought not to shove the whole thing in my mouth.

Pacing myself, I swallowed mouthful after mouthful as slowly as I could. Vincent sat in his chair again, and folded his hands on the table in front of him.

"I want to know how you trained the Nevermores. It is more than apparent that your techniques are better than any I've implemented so far."

"Torture rarely works on animals," Clark said. "Especially intelligent ones. I already told you that."

Vincent stiffened. "Clark. You aren't needed here."

Clark didn't move.

Now that was interesting.

I took another bite before answering. I needed to give myself more time to come up with an answer that would satisfy Vincent. I was pretty sure telling him "I don't know" wasn't going to cut it.

I pointed my spoon at the man sitting across from me. "How do I know you're telling the truth about the cure? Have you seen any Nevermores turned back into humans?"

Vincent's jaw tightened. "Are you calling me a liar? Are you questioning my integrity?"

I put both hands on the table, flat with my palms down. "Are you serious? You freely admit to torturing Nevermores. You've threatened my life, the life of my unborn child," Clark jerked at that, "and my husband's life. You can't seriously think I'm going to just believe whatever comes out of your mouth."

I cleared my throat and forced down another mouthful of soup. Suddenly, it didn't taste so good. "I'm asking for something that any reasonable person would. You can't make a claim like 'Nevermore can be cured' and then expect people to follow you blindly."

Behind me Green shifted his feet. I looked back at him. "Seriously?"

Vincent slapped his hands on the table. "Of course, they follow me. They've seen that living on their own is not possible. Outside this compound, death waits for them."

"I'm not going to attempt to train anything until you give me a reason. A real reason, not just your *word*."

The faintest flicker of a smile slipped across Clark's mouth. Apparently, he approved. Maybe he would be on my side like Green had said. I wouldn't count on it yet, though.

Vincent drew in a deep breath and leaned back in his chair. "Fine. We'll do this your way, for the moment. Let me give you a little chemistry lesson. How much do you know about the components of the Nevermore drug?"

Chewing on a bite of garlic bread, I thought back to the sheet my family doctor had given me on the breakdown of the drug.

"It's made from Scotch broom and there's dopamine in it. And something called tyramine, too, I think, but I'm not entirely clear on how that helps the drug work exactly," I said.

He wrote those drugs on the board in perfect capital letters and added a few I didn't recognize. He tapped each word with his chalk one at a time, like a teacher to a stubborn student.

"Genistin increases the calcium content in bones and prevents mass bone loss. Hence, the density of the Nevermores' bodies and the reason they avoid water. Sparteine and certain flavonoids deal with cardiovascular problems like arrhythmias, which has given them stronger hearts to pump blood faster. This aids not only in their speed, but also their decreased healing time." He paused and I nodded at him to continue.

"Dopamine, when released in the proper form, crosses the blood-brain barrier and makes immense improvements and even prevents Parkinson's disease." Vincent paused and frowned at me. "Dopamine is also released as a reward when we consume food or have sex. The way it is working in the Nevermores, it is giving them a high every time they eat. They are addicts, if you will."

"What about tyramine?" I asked, caught up in the intricacies of a drug that I had almost taken. I'd done my homework, but not to this level of a breakdown. I'd known the results of the drug, or thought I did, and hadn't gone further than that.

Vincent nodded again with a bare twist of his lips. I found myself almost smiling with pleasure that I'd asked a good question. This was dangerous. I did not want to fall into the role of trying to make him happy with me. No, that wouldn't help Bastian or me.

"Tyramine helps to release the body's stores of dopamine. That only adds to the feel-good factor the drug induces."

Another tap on the chalkboard brought my eyes back to center. Vincent continued his explanation. "Tyramine can also affect blood pressure, regulating it, which goes hand in hand with improvements of heart health. Again, this only adds to the increased ability to heal and the speed which they have."

I frowned. "But none of that has anything to do with weight loss."

"You ask good questions, Mara. You remind me of . . ." He stopped himself and his whole body stiffened for a moment. Fast enough that I wondered if I'd seen what I'd seen, he shook off whatever he was going to say. "That is the most incredible part when it comes to this drug. It wasn't designed for weight loss. It was designed for all these other things. But as the test subjects described their experiences of losing weight at a rapid pace, it became evident that the cocktail that damn scientist had mixed together forced the body's metabolism into overdrive."

"But then what happened to make them lose their minds, to go feral?" Despite the fact I hated him and all he'd done, I found myself wrapped up in the education he was giving me. I couldn't help but want to know what exactly had happened to Sebastian and all those people who took the Nevermore shot.

Vincent paced in front of the chalkboard, his hands once more clasped behind his back. Clark watched him with a distinct look of curiosity in his eyes. Apparently, I wasn't the only one getting something out of this.

"There are a great deal of toxins within *Cytisus scoparius* that were supposed to be eliminated. As the last reports told, they weren't because of the rapid pace of production. The checks and balances that kept the drug pure were ignored for the sake of greed."

Clark stepped forward. "But there were those who took the drug in the initial phase that also turned. Not all of them, but some."

My eyes widened, my food forgotten. "How the hell did it get through all the regulations then?"

"It took longer to turn them than the six weeks the later drug gave," Clark said. "Those who took early variations had up to six months, a few of them even eight months before they turned. And again, it wasn't all of them."

Vincent nodded. "The first batch was bad, batches three through five were fine, and then it went into mass production. And we all know what happened there."

"How do you know all these details? Are you a scientist?" I stared at him as my brain processed everything I was learning.

Vincent shook his head. "No, I'm no scientist. But I was there when the drug was being produced in the early stages. I applied myself to learning all I could about it when it was given to someone I cared about. Particularly when it became apparent the drug was not what it was supposed to be."

He turned to the chalkboard and continued as though Clark and I hadn't interrupted him.

"The very things that were meant to help those who took the drug had side effects, too, as we've all seen. The components, every one of them, had a flip side, a dark side, if you will." He made small arrows to and from each component to a big ugly *X* he slashed onto the board. Again he began to pace the room.

"Genistin stimulates breast cancer; I've not seen too many cases, but there are several Nevermores we have disposed of that had massive tumors hanging off their chests—so large, in fact, that they had difficulty standing upright."

I didn't know what to say; that was an image that came all too easily to my mind.

"The poison within the broom leaves the person with numb hands and feet, and that numbness travels up through their limbs. I believe this is why they are unable to climb, or at least, a contributing factor. The fine motor skills also seem to be greatly damaged; again, I believe this to be some of the toxins causing blockages." He stopped his pacing and leaned against the table to stare at me, his intensity unnerving.

I didn't want to tell him that I'd seen the Nevermores' ability with fine motor skills changing and improving.

He flicked his fingers on the table, drumming them lightly. "The flavonoids, they are carcinogenic in the right parameters and some of those seem to be met in certain patients. Again, tumors, skin cancer, and the like have been apparent on a number of them, eating away until their packs turn on them and kill them."

I couldn't even pretend to eat any more. The images were all too clear in my mind. "What about their minds, then? They are intelligent, even you can see that. How is all this affecting them?"

To my relief, he shook his head. "The initial thought that the brain was actually being attacked by the Nevermore drug and eaten away was incorrect. Parts of the cerebrum is being depressed while other parts are being stimulated. Thus we get the effect of the Nevermores. Humans gone feral." He put the chalk on the table and placed his hands beside it.

"Great as this information is," I said, "it still doesn't prove you are any closer to a cure than my dog is to growing wings and flying away."

Vincent raised an eyebrow at me and hit a button on the desk. He leaned over the button.

"Bring Adam and Eve in."

We waited a few minutes before a door to the left of me slid open. A single guard came in along with a woman and man dressed in what looked like bed sheets. They stumbled slightly in front of him, shuffling their feet slowly. I stared hard at them because I wasn't entirely sure I could be seeing what I was seeing.

"They are perfectly safe," Vincent said. "Go ahead." He motioned at me with both hands as if shooing me away.

I stood and cautiously walked closer to the pair to get a better look at them.

Their eyes were yellow, but the horizontal slit that was so disturbing had blended back into a proper round human iris. Their skin was still speckled here and there with the broom flower patterning that was so common on the Nevermores, but their skin itself was no longer yellow.

Something was still off, though, and I finally put my finger on it. I stared hard at them and they looked through me, as if I didn't exist.

That was it. The flat, dead gaze that stared out of their faces, the 'no vacancy' that should have been a blinking sign above their heads. I waved my hand in front of their faces and snapped my fingers a few times.

"They aren't in there anymore, are they?"

"Adam and Eve were injected with one of the earlier formulas of the reversal drug. We broke into Donavan's compound before he made better arrangements for protection." Vincent came around to my side of the table. "Because the toxin from the *Cytisus scoparius* depressed parts of the cerebrum that make us human in these two, it didn't leave any pathways for their brains to re-connect. Months as Nevermores and they no longer know themselves, or much of their surroundings for that matter. But they are no longer monsters. They are, for all intents and purposes, safe."

I backed away from them. "That doesn't make me want to give the formula to Sebastian."

Vincent stepped behind me and put his hands on my shoulders, squeezing the bones until they ground against one another.

"What is better, a man you can trust in your bed—simple, but safe—or an animal who is unpredictable, ready to tear your throat out at the slightest provocation? I saw him attack you outside your home, saw the terror it inspired in you. At least *this* way, you could have him with you. They are unpredictable, Mara. Today, he might protect you. Tomorrow, he could try to tear your throat out."

I stared at the couple. A thin line of drool formed from the woman's mouth and hung from her bottom lip, dropping until it reached the sheet over her breast. Which would be better? A vegetable, unable to communicate in any way? Or a monster, at least still aware of me and the past we shared?

I already knew I didn't really have a choice when it came to helping Vincent.

I would do what I had to do to keep Sebastian, our

child, and myself safe, no matter what. But I would never let Sebastian take this reversal drug. I could never live with myself knowing I'd taken what was left of his mind.

CHAPTER SIXTEEN

Mara

Adam and Eve were escorted out and Vincent pushed a sheet of paper toward me.

"This is what I want you to train the Nevermores to do. They must be able to follow these simple commands if we are to take Donavan's compound and, by taking it, take control of the cure."

I read the list on the paper out loud. "Attack, kill, left, right, forward, back, halt, quiet, loud."

I thought for a minute. The paper crinkled as I tightened my hand on it. "How do you think the Nevermores will help you take this compound, exactly?"

"That is none of your business. Your job is to train them." His words were sharp and I could see I had pushed him to the edge.

Time to make a tactful retreat. "Will you give me what I ask for to train them?"

Vincent frowned and shook his head. "Won't they just listen to you?"

I shrugged and glanced at the paper. "Maybe? I only know that with Scout, I used food to gain his trust. And as you pointed out, they are all practically addicts when it comes to food."

He shook his head. "We can't spare any extra food. We are on rations as it is."

"Then I'm not sure how well this will go," I said, clenching the paper in my fingers.

Vincent snorted and slapped his hand on the table. His eyes narrowed as he stared me down. "Figure it out, Mara, or I will see you shot on the post. But not before I eviscerate your husband and feed his liver to the crows."

Nausea rolled through me hot and fast. Not because of his words, but because the food that I'd been without for too long wasn't getting along with my stomach.

"I'm going to puke," I whispered.

Vincent curled his lip up and half closed his eyes. "You are so weak."

I didn't care what he thought at that moment. I lunged for the waste basket and caught the edge of it as the chicken noodle soup came back up, most of the noodles still intact. I heaved until my stomach was empty and then some more as if my body wanted to make sure there was nothing of Vincent's left in there.

"Get her out of here," Vincent snapped. "And take that damn basket."

Hands circled around my waist and lifted me to my feet.

128

"Don't touch my stomach," I managed to say right before another dry heave racked my body. The hands steadied me and helped me out the door.

A glance up when I finally got control of myself showed me Clark as my escort. That was a surprise; I'd assumed Green was assigned to me.

We made our way through the bunker to a hallway lined with doors back to the room where Green and I had left Missy. She bounced up and down when she saw me, a whine escaping her with her excitement.

"Good girl." I rubbed a hand over her head.

The room was compact, tidy, and even had a real bed, along with a small desk, chair, and a tiny closet. Not that I had anything to put in the closet, but I suppose it was a nice touch.

"Here, this is where you'll stay. I'll come get you in a few hours for your first session training the Nevermores," Clark said.

I lay down on the bed, groaning with relief, while my head spun. "Can I have some water, at least?"

"Sure." The door closed behind him and I closed my eyes and put a hand to my belly. I wasn't cramping, so I was pretty sure it wasn't a miscarriage, but the baby was not happy with the soup. Just the thought of the noodles made me gag again. Missy gave a soft woof a split second before the door opened and Clark stepped back in. He set a large plastic tumbler of water on my side table. "Here, you can have as much water as you want, but everything else is on rations."

"I don't want to eat anything unless it's bread or crackers," I said and then took a sip of water. It washed away the puke taste a little, which was a small improvement. I lay back on the bed and threw my arm over my eyes. For a moment, I wanted to believe I was somewhere else. Anywhere but here.

"Be careful with Vincent," Clark said.

I didn't remove my arm from my face. "I won't let him hurt me or Bastian if I can do anything about it."

"Bastian isn't your husband anymore. I give you full points for being loyal, but he isn't in there. I know better than anyone else."

I dropped my arm from my face. "Your wife?"

His face was a careful blank. "Is one of them. Love isn't enough. Not with this drug." He said nothing more, turned, and walked away.

He closed the door behind him with a hard click.

I patted the bed and Missy jumped up with me. I needed to sleep. I was exhausted and knew *that* would only add to the nausea. With Missy warm against me, and fatigue from the puking, I fell asleep within minutes.

I dreamt of the beach again. But this time, it was Clark with me, holding my hand, staring into my face, his eyes soft, a smile at the corner of his lips.

"Stay with me, Mara," he whispered into my ear as he wrapped his arms around my waist.

"I can't," I pulled away from him. "I love Sebastian."

"He's a monster. He can't love you back. They aren't capable."

I shook my head, which made my hair swing around my face, hiding the scene from me. "No, he does love me. You don't know him!"

Hands touched me and I flinched and found myself looking into Sebastian's face.

"Babe," he said, his lips in my hair, his words muffled, "I don't know how much longer I can hang on. The Nevermores call to me stronger than ever. I want you to be safe. I want to know you will survive."

"Then stay with me, Bastian, you can help me stay safe," I begged. "Don't go."

"He's right. I'm afraid I'll hurt you. I'm afraid I'll forget who I am and—" Bastian let go of me and pushed me towards Clark.

"No! Please, stop!" I yelled. I fought, but Clark held me tightly as again I watched Sebastian disappear from view.

"I promise you, I will never stop loving him." I pulled hard, doing all I could to get Clark to drop his arms.

He let me go as I fought his hold, and I tumbled to the hard-packed sand.

I woke with a start, the blanket tangled around me, soaked through with sweat. I sat up and grabbed for the glass of water still on the side table. I gulped it back and eased the dry ache in my throat. "I promise," I whispered into the semi-darkness as I clutched the glass. "I promise."

CHAPTER SEVENTEEN

Sebastian

he dream held me tightly as I walked away from Mara. Her cries followed me as I left her with Clark. He would be better, safer for her, and that was all I'd ever wanted. I wanted her to be safe, to not be afraid.

My feet were heavy as I kept moving in the opposite direction. The beach sand shifted and changed into heavy rocks and pebbles that bit at my feet. I lifted my eyes and the tropical paradise had faded into the thick undergrowth of the island I called home. Evergreen trees and thick bush lined the edges of the beach, dotting it with color.

From between the trunks, faces peered, and slowly a pack of Nevermores slid from the forest, moving toward me. I stopped where I was and my feet sunk as though I were on quicksand and not pebbles. I sucked in a sharp breath as the smooth stones bubbled up around me and drew me down. I jerked to one side but the movement only sent me deeper, deeper until I was up to my jaw line, my entire body encased in the earth.

"Come with us. We can save you."

My eyes watered as I stared into the painfully bright blue sky. A figure stepped into my line of vision, blocking some of the sun's rays. Female, but not Jessica. I frowned and her strength washed over me, urging me to listen to her. Her confidence became mine and I wanted what she would offer, felt it to the marrow of my bones.

Her hand held steady, beckoning. "Come with us. You are one of us. Leave her behind. As long as you hold to her, you are not one of us."

This was a hand that would pull me to safety. She was strong, and the pack behind her carried that same strength. The call of her voice and the belief in it . . . I lifted my arm an inch, then dropped it with a thud to the rocks. I couldn't do it. I couldn't leave Mara, even knowing there was someone else who would watch over her.

The ground opened up and swallowed me whole, rocks careening all around me, battering me.

I broke from the dream with a jerk, which slammed my hand into the concrete wall of the cage. I tucked myself into a ball, cradling the hand I'd smashed reflexively.

That I'd even been asleep was a bit of a shock. Fatigue had washed through me with a suddenness that had left my legs shaking. I'd lain down and fallen asleep in minutes. I rubbed a hand over my face and head as if I could scrub away the image of Clark holding her. As if I could wash away the sound of her crying for me. I shook my head, but the dream had its hooks into me.

You share her dreams now.

I lifted my head slowly. That was a new voice. It could only mean the Alpha male had chosen to finally speak to me.

A small part of my brain thought perhaps he would work with me, and together we could break free of this place.

The rest of my mind pointed out that he'd been trying to control me using the other Nevermores' mind speak. Still, the fact that he knew I'd been dreaming and that Mara had been there made me curious enough to overcome any reservations I had.

I do not know that her dreams are mine.

A laugh echoed down the hall between us. I moved to the front of my cage and leaned into it.

An arm pushed out from between the bars of the cage at the far end of the hall. The fingers made a sweeping motion, as if beckoning me.

I see her dreams, too. She is . . . not like us, but like us. It makes her vulnerable. It changes her.

Fear, sudden and lancing like a hot poker, coursed through me. Had Mara taken Nevermore? Was she changing?

Could someone here have forced it on her? That thought took root and I could see all too easily the way it could have happened. How Vincent tied her down and forced the drug on her.

No, I don't think that will happen.

I lifted my head. *How do you know?*

The hand flicked again, this time in a rolling motion back and forth. *I am an Alpha. I hear her thoughts.*

That did not tell me anything. I leaned against the bars and closed my eyes. Actively searching for the thoughts of someone was not something I'd done. But if the other Alpha could sense Mara, then I should be able to as well.

Images flickered and danced through my mind from the other Nevermores. The desire mostly for food was at the front of their wants, but there were other things too. To be free, to be with the rest of their packs, to . . . take vengeance on the men who'd captured them. I steered away from those thoughts.

Slowly, carefully I picked my way through to the faintest of images. Ones that if I hadn't been looking for, I wasn't sure I would see at all.

Fear and determination hovered around her. The dog was with her and she clung to the animal for comfort. Two words came through clear now that I focused on her.

I promise.

What did she promise? And to whom? I pulled back from her thoughts, knowing they were almost too complex to read. They danced and jumped from place to place at a speed I struggled to follow. But now that I knew she was there, that I could find her, there was comfort in that thought.

You see? You just had to look, the Alpha sent to me.

I frowned. *Why are you helping me at all?*

There was a long pause, long enough I thought perhaps he wasn't going to answer. He rapped a knuckle on the bars. *Freeing ourselves from this place will take all of us. Even you.*

Even me. Like I wasn't a Nevermore.

He laughed again, softly, and with a sadness I didn't understand. The sound of it bounced around my brain, as if it would chase me. His voice in my head though was anything but soft. No, it was more confused than anything else.

That's just it . . . I don't think you are. But then, I'm not sure I am either.

CHAPTER EIGHTEEN

Mara

The dream left me shaken to the core. In part because it echoed my fears of losing Sebastian, but also because once I'd woken, it felt as though he were close to me, and if I just closed my eyes again I would feel his hand brush my cheek.

I buried my face in Missy's fur. This was not the time to lose my marbles.

"Time to plan, Missy, because I'm going to get us all killed if I don't do what Vincent wants." I needed to figure out what I was going to do with the Nevermores. Scout listened to me because he was afraid of Sebastian and because I bribed him with food. But the more I thought on it, the more I could see that trick had only worked because Scout was in the same pack as Sebastian—and he understood the hierarchy. I was the Alpha's mate, and that was all Scout had really needed.

I rubbed my hands over my eyes. "How am I going to do this?"

Missy butted me with her nose, demanding attention. I scratched the top of her head absentmindedly.

Though it was a long shot, perhaps Sebastian and I working together could do the same with the Nevermores here?

But how did I prove to the Nevermores that I was the Alpha's mate? The pack near our home had seen me with Bastian. He'd kept them away from me and guarded my gate.

Vincent's words about the Nevermores rolled around in my head. They were geared toward fulfilling their desire for food and sex, driven by the more primitive parts of their brains.

Monsters, but human underneath.

For a moment, I couldn't breathe as the solution came to me.

"Missy. I don't . . . I don't know if I can do it."

It meant putting on a show for the other Nevermores in the cells. To *show* them I was the mate of the Alpha in a most literal sense. I grabbed for my water glass, found it empty, and, trembling, poured myself another cup.

I gulped the water as my body shivered with an equal dose of fear . . . and desire. Sebastian and I had always had a healthy sex life, and neither of us were afraid to try new things. But . . . in front of the other Nevermores?

I wasn't sure I could do it. *It.* A nervous giggle escaped me, a hint of panic on the edge of the laughter.

A knock on my door made me jump and I spilled my water.

"Mara, I'm here to take you to the Nevermores," Green said.

I nodded, stood and snapped my fingers at Missy. She leapt from the bed and heeled to my left side.

"You can't take her."

"She needs to go out and relieve herself. Unless you want to tell Vincent she made a mess down here?"

Green glanced left and right quickly before he leaned in close. "What about that Nevermore up top?"

He had a point, but I would need time alone with Sebastian. "Keep her close to the bunker. She'll bark if Scout gets too close."

He pursed his lips but didn't argue with me. I wasn't sure that was a good thing. It made me think he'd gotten used to just doing what he was told and not thinking for himself.

We walked side by side through the halls, not talking. The dream and my subsequent plan left me jittery, as though I'd been drinking double-shot espressos. I ended up clasping my hands together in front of me to keep them from shaking.

"Green, I need to get in with Sebastian, right in his cell, if I'm to start the training. The others have to see me as his mate and see that he won't hurt me." I glanced at Green's profile as I spoke.

"That's not safe."

"It is for me." I lifted my chin.

Green seemed to struggle with something and finally blurted out, "He tried to strangle me the other day. After I saved him from Vincent, after I kept the sedatives from him, he tried to strangle me."

Shock coursed through me and I shook my head before his words really penetrated.

He glared at me. "Don't shake your head. He did try to."

"But he let go?"

Suddenly the bruises on his throat made sense. I'd thought they were from Vincent.

We were at the door that led down into the cell block. He stopped with his hand on the knob. "He let go."

"Why? What happened?"

"If I tell you, then you are going to think you are safe. And you aren't. Not with him. Not with any Nevermore. Not until we can find a proper cure."

"What stopped him?" I repeated.

Again he seemed to struggle, but finally he answered. "Your name. Your name stopped him."

I held my hand out, my decision made. "Give me the key, and take Missy for a walk. When you come back, call out from the top step."

"Why?"

I arched an eyebrow. "My training techniques are my own, thank you very much."

His eyes narrowed. "Don't do anything stupid, Mara. If he comes at you, get the hell out of that cell."

If he comes at me . . . I burst into laughter, the nervous giggles getting a hold of me. "Go. Just take Missy and go."

Green gave me one last look. "I don't like it."

"You don't have to. If he kills me, then I will own that." I clutched at the keys, the reality of what I was saying sinking into me.

"Vincent will kill Sebastian if—"

"Then at least we will be together." I turned from him and fumbled with the key in the lock. "Remember to call out before you come down the stairs."

"Mara . . ." He put a hand on my arm, stopping me. I didn't turn around.

"What?"

"There will be two guards with weapons stationed at the door when I leave. Don't try to break out."

I nodded and slid through the door, shutting it behind me before making my way down the stairs as quickly as I could. The sound of my heart pounding and the rapid breath in and out of my mouth was about all I could hear. I counted the cells, stopping in front of Sebastian's. There was no movement, no sign that he was even still in there. What if Vincent had moved him?

"Bastian?" I didn't dare even touch the bars of the cage on the chance that a different Nevermore was inside. No matter what Vincent thought, I was not fooling myself into thinking I had some strange connection with the Nevermores. Scout and Sebastian were different, special cases.

I tucked the keys into my back pocket. "Bastian, if you're in there, please, I need to speak to you." The double meaning to my words was not lost on me. Would he answer? Or would he turn his back on me like he had in the dream?

Finally, there was a shift in the shadows as he stood. He'd been sitting in the far corner, and as he drew closer, I could see that he . . . was not happy to see me. His brows were creased low and he did not even attempt a smile.

My heart hammered further, harder. I was betting all our lives on our love. That it was strong enough, that it would see us through this.

Monster or man, he was my husband, and I loved him with all my heart. Some of the fear began to slide from me as I held onto that truth. I reached back for the keys and brought them around to the cell.

"No." He grunted the word at me, and made a move as if to push me back.

"Don't you tell me no," I said as I got the key in the lock and twisted it hard. I pushed the door open before I changed my mind, slid through and shut the door behind me. Leaning against it, I stared up at him.

His jaw ticked and his eyes, that had seemed so strange at first, softened. He shook his head. Not being able to speak obviously frustrated him.

"Bastian, I need you to listen. Vincent, the one who tortured you—"

He let out a low, dangerous growl. I nodded. "He wants me to train the Nevermores."

Bastian frowned and shook his head again. Not possible, or he didn't understand?

"He will kill you, me, and our child if I don't do as he wants," I said softly.

A shudder rippled through him and his hands

clenched hard enough that his arms vibrated. I caught my bottom lip with my teeth.

"Bastian, the Nevermores here don't think I'm your mate, do they." Not a question.

His frown deepened and he shook his head slowly, then tipped it to one side. Why?

I drew in a deep breath. "They are all listening now? They hear us?"

A nod.

I swallowed hard. "And if you were to have sex with me now, here, would they accept me?"

His eyes flashed wide with surprise.

I couldn't help the heat on my cheeks, though it had been years since I'd felt this awkward about sex. Especially with Bastian.

"I trust you, Bastian. If you think it's a good idea, if you think that it will cement my place in the pack—"

He reached out and put his hand on the back of my neck, tugged me close to him and cut my sentence off most effectively.

"I mean, if you think," I whispered as I stared up at him, my hands pressed against his chest. I couldn't help but curl my fingers against his skin through a tear in his shirt, which only drew a low growl out of his mouth.

My breathing and heart rate climbed yet again, but for a whole new reason.

He tugged me backward into the shadows so there was no more seeing him. Just feeling.

And he was my husband, the man I loved with every fiber of my being. A tear slipped down my cheek and he caught it on the edge of his finger, then brought it to his lips.

There was a sudden cry of Nevermores around us and he lifted one hand into the air. They fell silent, though how they knew . . . I had no idea.

He pulled me back until we were against the far wall and he slid down, taking me with him. I moved with him, let his hands guide me until I sat on his lap, my knees on either side of his thighs. I wrapped my arms around him, breathing in the scent that was still him, just wilder, raw and untamed.

"I've missed you so much." I fought the tears that wanted to come. My damn hormones were all over the map.

He groaned as he pressed his mouth to the hollow of my throat and licked at my skin before pulling at it lightly with his teeth. A shiver of desire rippled through me, scattering the tears like leaves before a storm.

I slid my hands up his arms, reveling in rock-hard muscles and the smooth contours of his body, then up his neck to cup his face and bring his lips to mine. Slowly. Carefully. Like a first kiss all over again.

Our breath mingled, danced across our lips, and we leaned toward each other at the same time.

While the hope was that this would help me train the pack and gain their respect and trust, there was another reason for it too. I missed him. I missed his touch, and feel of him next to me. I missed his laughter and the snort he gave when he thought I was being ridiculous. I missed hearing him call me 'babe' and I missed not being able to share the subtle changes in my body with him. I wanted my husband back, and I was ready to admit that I would take him however that meant.

Man or monster, he was mine, and I loved him.

The taste of our last kiss, bittersweet and salted with tears . . . I did not want that to be the last memory I had of his touch. It haunted my heart, and I wanted nothing more than to erase it with something better. Something . . . alive.

I tipped my head, angling for a deeper kiss as I tightened my arms around his neck. Our tongues touched, once, twice, and then it was on like there'd never been a moment we'd been apart.

A rumble started deep in his belly, the vibration of it rolling through me which only set me to squirming in his lap. He grabbed my hips and held me still as he pulled me tightly against his arousal, pressing himself against me, grinding his hips upward. Clothes between us still, I struggled to keep myself from losing my control.

I groaned and he swallowed the noise as he kissed me hard, his mouth demanding a surrender that I gave freely. Hot, wet kisses exploded between us as we fought to cover each other with the love we'd always had. I kissed his cheeks, and eyes, neck and chest, then back to his mouth.

"I love you."

"Always," he whispered back and my heart broke, shattering as I fell into a sob against him. He held me up, pushed me gently back, but I shook my head.

"Don't stop. Please."

I struggled out of my shirt, and Sebastian slid his hands up my torso to cup my swollen breasts. He bent his head to capture a nipple in his mouth, suckling and teasing at it 'til I cried out. My hands tangled in his hair and I guided him to the other nipple, relishing in the passion behind each touch, each brush of skin against skin. For the first time, there was no allergic reaction to his saliva, no slow-burning fever that would leave me itching and confounded. There were only the rolling sensations between us as our skin heated, slicked, with desire and need. With love.

Sebastian growled softly and wrapped one arm around me. With an ease that surprised me, he stood, holding me in the air tightly against his body.

I pushed away from him, stood back, and slid out of my pants. But in the darkness, I couldn't see him and I held out a hand, waiting for him to find me again.

His hand caught around my wrist and he drew me slowly forward. I lifted my hands, slid them up his body until I cupped his face.

A small part of my brain whispered that I'd left the key in my pants pocket somewhere in the darkness, that if I needed to get away there would be no hope. But I'd already accepted that whatever came of this, it was my fate. Either I was with Sebastian or he was lost to me forever. I would rather die by his hand than Vincent's.

With a quick jerk, Sebastian yanked me into his arms so my legs straddled him. I sucked in a sharp gasp.

"Benefits to added strength, I see." I couldn't help it, that was our way. To tease and love at the same time.

A low chuckle rumbled out of him but it faded as the tip of his hardness brushed over my opening. I clung to his shoulders and tried to shimmy my hips closer, desire raging through me like I'd never had before. He had both hands on my ass, holding me up and tightly to him.

"Bastian, please." I was ready to beg if I had to. I arched as he rubbed across my sweet spot, back and forth, over and over again, his hips moving in a steady rhythm.

His breath was hot on my collarbone as I groaned and clung to him, wanting him with a fierceness I'm not sure I'd ever felt before. Knowing that I'd almost lost him once completely from the shot, and then a second time to Jessica. He was mine.

I would not lose him again.

As my breathing increased and my body began to clench, he slid into me, rock hard and throbbing with his own desire. A single thrust and he was fully inside me. I let out a cry that he partially captured with his mouth, our tongues tangled, and breath came in gasps and pants.

Together, we found a rhythm, our bodies remembering each other with a natural ease. We rocked hard against the desire that ripped through us, marked us once more as its captives. Every brush of skin on skin sent a higher spiral of pleasure through me until I could hold the sound in no longer.

Bastian's own growls filled the air as we stumbled to the wall and he leaned me hard against the stone. The shock of the cold against my back and the heat of Bastian at my front sent a sharp gasp out of my mouth that turned into a moan.

With a crashing spasm, my peak took me and sent me spinning out of control. Bastian's body thrust into mine, his rhythm gone as he sought his own climax. Our breath lost sync as the craving for each other took over. Even as we came down from the high, our hands coasted over hot, flushed skin, smoothing away the sweat.

Panting hard, Sebastian held me close and moved us back to the corner where he'd sat when I'd come in. I didn't want to let go of him, not yet. I wanted this closeness, to feel him in me, his body still throbbing with pent-up need. As he sat, I started to move, shifting my hips in a seductive dance, as I pressed my breasts against his chest and let my nipples brush along his hardened skin.

His hands circled my waist and he helped me find a decadent pace so slow that it brought us both near to writhing once more. Sebastian bent his head and pulled a gasp out of me as he suckled my breasts while our hips still danced to their own song. With his touch and tongue and the feel of him deep within me, my body constricted, quickly peaking again. Groaning, I didn't fight the noises or try to hold off the pleasure. The spasms of my muscles brought him along with me, driving us high and leaving us gasping for air.

Exhausted, I leaned my naked and sweating body

against his as his hands roved over my back. Carefully he slipped one between us and settled it on my belly bump. Carefully, as if he wasn't quite sure if he should, he cupped it. A lump rose in my throat, and I knew that no matter what happened, no matter who stood between us, this love could never be taken from us.

"I love you, Sebastian. I don't care about the changes in you. Love can make this work. Somehow," I said. I kissed his lips softly, and then rested my head on his shoulder.

"Love, too," he whispered into my ear just before he licked the sweat from the side of my neck and pulled me back under a tidal wave of desire.

CHAPTER NINETEEN

Sebastian

I held onto her as long as I could, let her smell and touch take me away from the place we were, from the Nevermores on the other side of the wall, from the fears that pushed in on all sides. This was my life. She was where I would stand, no matter what came. A sigh slid out of me as I watched her pull her clothes on.

"Green will be back for me soon." She dug around in her pocket and pulled out the keys. I stood and yanked my shirt and pants on. My fingers fumbled, but I managed to do it. She noticed right away.

"You're getting more mobility in your fingers, aren't you?"

I nodded.

She bit her lower lip and stared at the keys in her hands. "There are guards waiting up top with guns, or I would say we should just make a run for it."

I shook my head, wanting desperately to convey

to her that there would be another way. I wasn't sure how, only I knew that something would come. A little patience and we'd find a path out of this place together.

The thought warmed me even as she kissed me goodbye and slid out of the cell. She paused as she shut the door. "Do you think . . . that it worked? Do you think they will see me as your mate now?"

I went to the bars and grasped them and closed my eyes. I filtered through the images of the other Nevermores, but specifically the other male Alpha. His thoughts were guarded, but I prodded at him, making him take notice of me when he tried to block me out.

She is my mate. Is she safe?

His thought came slowly, as if he were weighing each image.

Perhaps. Her chances are better now than before. She is clever.

I opened my eyes and struggled to form the word I looked for. "Better."

She smiled and the place didn't seem so dark. "I'll take it."

The sound of the door above opening snapped my head up. A voice called down. "Mara, you're out of time."

She turned her head and called back, "Coming."

Her hand reached through and she touched my chest over my heart. "We'll find a way out. I promise."

And then she was gone and I was alone once more

with the Nevermores around me. I kept their images out for the most part until I saw something new.

Flickers of Nevermores I didn't know—ones not in the cells—were at the edges of my mind. I focused on them as I'd focused on Mara to listen to her thoughts and the images became clearer, opening to me.

These new Nevermores, they roamed around, hungry and lusting after food and the men inside the compound. I jerked upright and sucked in a sharp breath. The Nevermores were planning an attack on the men the minute they stepped outside, and there were enough of them to do serious damage.

They were swarming, packing, and calling all the Nevermores they could to reinforce them. Panic clawed at me. Even I knew that being my mate would not save Mara from that sort of blood lust. Maybe if I was with her, I could keep her free of them, but in the middle of it?

I grabbed at the bars and sent a strong image to the other Alpha.

The other Nevermores are planning to take over this pack.

Yes.

I gripped the bars tighter. *Give me a chance to get my mate first.*

Silence met my request and I snarled, letting a roar of frustration bellow out of me.

The other Nevermores shifted away from me and a few laughed. The Alpha grunted.

I promise nothing.

And it was then that he let me in and I saw what Vincent had done to him. Both his feet had been removed at the ankle, leaving nothing but bloodied stumps.

I recoiled and stumbled away from the cage and the bars. We were trapped and at the mercy of a monster.

CHAPTER TWENTY

Mara

The next day, I stood in front of Vincent while he read the list of things I would need to train the Nevermores. I'd pored over it most of the night. I'd paced my room with a pen in my mouth and Missy at my heels as I'd tried to think of the easiest way to test the theory that the other Nevermores would listen. But I also needed space so that I could see more of the terrain—in other words, I needed to see if there was a weak spot in Vincent's barracks. A weak place I could exploit.

His eyes flickered over the first few items. A few loaves of bread. A couple of blankets. But it was the last bit that sent his eyebrows up to his hairline. "You want to set them loose in the rifle range? I don't see how this is going to train them unless we are shooting *at* them. Is that going to be your plan of attack? Shoot them until the rest cower? Because I will tell you right now, that doesn't work."

I shook my head and tucked the scarf Green had given me around my neck a little tighter to hide Sebastian's love bites.

Green had taken one look at me when I'd reached the top of the stairs and had gone pale. "You can't let Vincent know."

He'd dug around in the box of leftover clothes until he found a suitable scarf.

Green was right—no one else needed to know how deep my connection to Sebastian still was. It would do me no good to have Vincent think I was willing to lay my body on the line to make things happen. For all I knew, he would consider it open game on me and try to make me take the place of woman he'd killed. I suppressed a shiver of revulsion as I thought of Fran, a woman who'd been forced into servicing the officers and was killed when she stood up for herself. I couldn't let Vincent think of me in a sexual way.

I cleared my throat and tapped the notes I'd put at the bottom of the list of things I wanted to use in my training of the Nevermores. "I need to set up a simulation of how a real pack would exist. They have a hierarchy and I need to be a part of it if you want this to have even a chance of working. In the cells they are divided."

Vincent grunted and continued to look the paper over. "As a pack, they are stronger."

"But I can't prove to you I can control them, train them, if they aren't in pack formation. Can I?" My logic was sound. I was sure of it. I'd tried to poke holes in it all night.

Vincent folded the paper and tucked it into the front pocket of his ugly army green shirt.

"I'll have Clark and the other boys round up the Nevermores we have and put them in there."

I leaned forward. "No, that's not what I asked for. All of them except Sebastian go out to the range. We have to hold him back 'til the rest of the males have fought it out."

"Why, you don't want him to prove himself?" He smiled and it was not a nice smile. A twist of panic doubled over on itself inside my belly.

"I need him to be the pack leader if we are going to have a chance—"

"Then he will go out with the rest. Either he will survive or he won't. That's life now, Mara."

I gripped the edge of the table as the room swayed a little. "And if I can't train them without him?"

"Then you die, too. I thought I already made this clear? Failure is not an option, Mara." He leaned over and pushed his intercom button. "Round up *all*," he looked at me, "the Nevermores and put them in the rifle range. Be sure to catch the one wandering around outside and throw him in there, too."

He stared at me, a wrinkle in between his eyes that drew tighter the longer he stared. I forced myself to hold still and not fidget under his steady gaze. His eyes dipped to the scarf wrapped around my neck. I arched an eyebrow, a mixture of anger and fear making me brassy. "What?"

"You seem to have quite the glow about you. I must assume you truly . . . *enjoyed* . . . your visit with

Sebastian." The tip of his tongue slid out along the edge of his mouth. I caught the shudder that wanted to ripple through me. God help me, did he have a video on the cells?

A hot flush spread up my neck to my cheeks, giving any pretence away. I took a deep breath and squared my shoulders. I would not cower, or be ashamed. "He's my husband. I love him. What do you want?"

"I have no doubt of that, Mara." Vincent let out a sigh. "Only love can make you do stupid things like take your clothes off with a monster who could kill you with one hand."

The flush turned into a white hot anger. "Sebastian—"

He waved his hand. "Isn't like the others. I have heard enough of that line to make me sick."

Vincent nodded and sat on the edge of the table. "My Juliana, she was forced to take the Nevermore shot. Even as a monster, I would still have her in my life. Though I'd likely have to tie her up to enjoy her favors once more." There was a gleam in his eye that made me think that tying up his love and taking her without consent didn't really bother him.

Curiosity got the better of me. "What happened to her?"

Vincent took a deep breath and let it out slowly as he sank into his chair. "Donavan forced her to take the shot, made her take it, and then locked her away in a cage when she became a monster. He's only doing it to hurt me now. He doesn't care for her. It's why I am going to make him pay."

"And use the monsters—like Juliana turned into—to do it," I said softly. The irony was not lost on me. Though, I didn't think it was smart. Donavan was the one trying to find the cure. Helping him would be the smartest thing to do. Not killing him.

Vincent leaned forward, his eyes hard. "You have a job to do, so do it. Train the Nevermores. Here," he handed me a fresh pad of paper and a pen. "I have rounds to do. I want a detailed list of how long it will take to get the Nevermores working on command. How you see this training progressing, as well as any information you can give me on the Nevermores. Observations, abilities, weaknesses. Including their likes," he reached out and snatched the scarf off my neck, "and dislikes."

He strode around the desk and dropped it into my lap. "Cover your neck up. You'll set my men off seeing those bites."

I grabbed at the blue material. The door slammed behind me. "Then why'd you take it off, you ass!" I snapped.

I sat for a moment and stared at the pad of paper. I tapped my pen on the top of the page, feeling as though I were back in school taking a pop quiz. Frustrated, I stood and paced the room. I needed to move, to get my thoughts in order. I found myself in front of the single bookshelf in the room. My fingers trailed along the spines. Would they give me insight to the dictator who held my life, and the life of my tiny family, in his hands? Would they help me figure a way out of this mess?

Unfortunately for me there was nothing of consequence that I could see. Just a mixed bag of novels, non-fiction, and how-to manuals. My fingers brushed a thin volume that was light pink, and tucked between two thick dark green army manuals. The pale color didn't jibe with the rest of the books. My heart hiccupped as my fingers paused on the pink spine. I slowly pulled it out.

In a beautiful scrawl was a single name written in cursive on the cover.

Juliana.

Could it be her journal? Unable to restrain myself, I let the book fall open in my hands and started to read. Chills rippled through me as the words painted a very different picture than the one Vincent was trying to feed me.

Vincent followed me home again. He said that Donny sent him, but Donny already told me that Vincent had been sacked. I managed to keep him out of the house, but only just barely. He had his foot in the door and if Mrs. Chester from across the street hadn't popped out and waved I'm not sure he would have stopped.

I flipped a few pages.

The bruises are almost healed. The police say that a restraining order will help but I'm not sure it will. Donny is so busy with his new breakthrough I don't want to worry him.

"Tell your husband, tell him," I whispered to the pages. I flipped a couple of more.

Vincent raped me last night.

I flipped one more, the last page in the book.

Donny can never know what happened.

I didn't hear the door behind me open.

"What the hell are you doing?" Vincent screamed.

I dropped the journal and spun to face him. I was caught red-handed and didn't have the words to stop him.

Vincent rushed me and I ran around the large table, keeping distance between us.

"You bitch, I'll kill you!" he snarled. "I'll gut you like a fish and feed the pieces to your husband!"

I did the only thing I could. I lied. "I believe you, Vincent! Donavan wasn't the one she loved, it was you. I'm a woman. I can see what she was trying to say in that journal."

He stopped at the opposite side of the table from me. "What?"

I was breathing hard, but I forced the words out, knowing they might save me. "Juliana was in love with you. That's what I saw when I read her words. She didn't want to be with Donavan, but he made her stay. He . . . hurt her."

Vincent stood, squaring his shoulders. For the first time, I saw something flicker in his eyes that scared me more than the anger.

Madness.

He straightened his clothes, breathing hard. "You should never have read her journal."

I nodded. "I know. I didn't realize what it was. But

then I saw . . . as I read her words. . . that you and I are in the same position really."

Vincent's eyes narrowed and I rushed on, spinning the lies as fast as I dared, hoping he could believe me. "You love Juliana, but she was taken away by the Nevermore shot. We should be working together, to find a cure for her and Sebastian."

His jaw twitched. "The Nevermores have been rounded up and put in the rifle range. I suggest you leave now and deal with their training."

I backed away from him, my hands finding the doorknob by feel alone.   Instinct told me that turning my back on him right then would be deadly.

Once out the door, I turned and walked as fast as I dared in the dim tunnels. I hit dead ends twice before I stumbled into the kitchen. My mind raced with what I'd learned. At the moment, though, there was nothing I could do about it. I had to focus on keeping myself and Sebastian alive, which meant training the Nevermores.

There was no one in the kitchen, so I slipped in, thinking about Sebastian and Scout, how hungry they must be. It didn't matter that they didn't seem to need the food to survive; I wanted them to have something. I couldn't be sure that Vincent would keep his word about the food and blankets. In fact, I seriously doubted it. I scrambled to keep my hands busy, shaking as they were. Hurried to do anything that would keep my mind off what I'd read in the journal.

This was not the time to be thinking about what a psycho Vincent was.

In the second cupboard, I found a loaf of stale bread, with faint green mold growing on the edges. It would have to do, and besides, I'd seen Scout eat a human body. I doubted he would mind a little bacterial culture. That was the only useful food I found besides a can of some indistinguishable food. I shook it, but it didn't really matter since I didn't have a can opener. I left the can behind and tucked the loaf under my arm.

It only occurred to me then that this was the first time I'd not had an escort or guard. I froze where I was and listened for running footsteps.

Nothing. Of course, it would take all the men to get the Nevermores to the rifle range. Which left no one to watch over me. I went through the kitchen more slowly, no longer looking for food.

A solid knife beckoned to me from a drawer I opened. I pulled it out and held it up to the light. Five inches long with a narrow black handle, the blade was nicked at the tip like someone had tried to use it as a pry bar on some unwilling coconut. I put the loaf of bread on the counter and continued to search for anything that might help.

Nothing else was small enough that I could take. As it was, the knife was going to be tricky.

"What the hell am I going to do with it?" I was not so stupid as to think Vincent or his men would allow me to keep the knife if they saw me with it. I held the knife in one hand and the bread in the other. I could stick the knife in the bread loaf, but if I had to throw the loaf to the Nevermores, there went my one weapon.

I settled for tucking the knife through the side of my belt, and untucking my shirt to cover it. Hardly perfect, but it was all I had.

The hallway past the kitchen was quiet as I stepped out. It was as if the men really had forgotten about me.

An image of Nevermores fighting, of screeching and biting, flickered through my mind as they pushed and shoved at each other. They were figuring out the order of where they belonged before the fights for Alpha began. What, how was it possible that I even knew that? I put a hand to my temple. My imagination was running away with me again.

I made my way down the hallway until I found my bedroom. I opened the door and Missy lifted her head from my pillow.

"Come on, girl. I need your help, too."

Missy leapt from the bed and heeled to my side. The two of us found the stairs that led up to the hatch that would let us outside. I paused with my hand on the metal handle. Sunlight, warm air, and freedom awaited us along with Sebastian and the Nevermores.

My mouth and throat were dry. "Here we go."

I pushed the door open. A soldier with a gun held loosely in his arms nodded to me as I stepped outside. Sunlight didn't flood in as I'd thought—rain did. A summer rainstorm filled the morning sky with dark, ominous clouds. A foreboding feeling hung over the open door.

"Where's the rifle range?" I asked the solider. I didn't recognize him from the trucks that had brought us in. Then again, I'd not really been taking much notice of facial details at that point.

"Follow the fence line north. You can't miss it."

Movement by my original barracks alerted me to Scout. Maybe Vincent's men hadn't had time to round him up. Or maybe he just kept eluding them. That was more likely.

Keeping my pace steady, I strode toward him. He had to come with us. It would be safer for Sebastian and me with Scout on our sides. Missy's hackles went up and she strutted in front of me.

The solider at the door shouted after me. "Hey, you're going the wrong way."

I didn't take my eyes off Scout. "I'll head that way in a minute."

Scout scrambled backward, falling over himself to keep distance between us. I pulled off a chunk of bread and held it out to him.

"You can have more, but only if you're good." I tried to keep my face and voice stern. Alpha like.

He squinted at me as if he was considering the offer. More likely, he was trying to figure out how to get the whole loaf of bread and maybe my hand along with it. He lifted his head and sniffed in my direction, then froze, a shudder rippling through his body. He shook his head once and then scratched at his left ear.

He seemed unsure of what to do exactly. With the hunk of bread in my hand, I touched my chest. "Alpha's mate."

He sniffed the air again and then slowly bobbed his head.

I smiled to myself. I deliberately hadn't showered after I'd made love to Sebastian. I wanted his scent on me, and from Scout's reaction, it was working. Scout knew I was Sebastian's mate in every way and that meant I held rank over the lowly Nevermore.

"Be good." I flipped the chunk of bread to him. He caught it and swallowed it in two bites. "Come on, we've got to go." I snapped my fingers like I often did for Missy. Scout, trembling, scuttled to my opposite side. He lowered his head, his spine curved in, completely submissive, not a single trace of predatory hunger. This was a good sign; my plan just might work after all.

Missy walked on my other side, shooting glances at Scout as he shot glances at her. Pack, we were all a pack, and I was going to make this work. "Be nice to Missy, too, Scout."

I wasn't sure he'd understand that complicated of a thought, but it was worth trying.

The three of us walked north along the fence line. The solider in front of the door stared with his mouth open.

I was making an impression at least. That had to bode in my favor.

A sudden thought hit me like a blow between the eyes. Did Vincent think I was just one of those who'd taken the Nevermore shot late and was just biding his time, using me before he killed me? No, no, it had been too long since the last shots were administered. He wouldn't think that.

Would he? He was not exactly in his right mind,

that much was clear. So there was a chance he just thought I was going to turn.

My stress levels shot through the roof. Why hadn't I thought of this before?

But I had no time to worry as the rifle range came into sight.

The range had a fence around it, separate from the perimeter fence. Nevermores milled about inside the range. Not one of them made a single sound despite the soldiers placed at intervals around the outside edge. What surprised me most was there was no fighting going on, no males vying for place in the pack. Several of the Nevermores had bruises and cuts, but they seemed to have settled. I shook my head. No, I had to have been imagining things before. There was no way I should have been able to know that the pack had been fighting when I couldn't see them. Sweat curled down the side of my face.

I did a quick sweep of the pack with my eyes. No Sebastian.

My heart picked up its pace. Did that mean he'd fallen? Was he forced in to fight his way to the top of the pack only to be . . . killed?

I placed a hand on Scout's head.

"No attacking." I patted him for good measure. He sat back on his heels and stared at the ground. Good enough. I did another quick head count while at the same time looking for my husband. There were at least thirty Nevermores inside the rifle range. I counted twenty-three men and seven women, including the heavily pregnant one.

Clark's ex-wife.

Speaking of Clark, he headed my way from the far side of the rifle range. "Now what, Mara? We've got them in here, and your man is waiting to be let in as you requested." His eyes dropped to Scout tucked up against my legs, and he froze, his eyes bugging out a little. "Holy shit. I didn't think you could do it."

Ignoring him, I asked my own question. "Where's Sebastian?"

As if my words had conjured them, three soldiers came out of the back side of the barracks with Sebastian bound and walking between them. They had a catchpole over his neck as though he were a rabid dog. Another catchpole held his right leg, and a third kept hold over his left wrist. The three soldiers used the leverage they had to keep him off balance, and that was about all they had going for them. Every step he lunged toward one of them and the others had to pull him back, saving their comrade. There was nothing human about Bastian in those moments.

"Bring him to me." Fear laced my words. I couldn't help it.

How do you love someone so much and yet still fear them, knowing they could turn on you in an instant? It was a terrible combination of emotions and they warred for my attention within my heart and mind.

Sebastian saw me and his struggling ceased as he got closer to me and Scout. His eyes softened and his growls subsided completely. It was a good sign, and the guards relaxed their grips on the poles. The rain came at us sideways, slicking everything including the catchpoles. I had a feeling that if Sebastian had really wanted to, he could have made the soldiers let go. He was holding back.

I put a hand on his arm and he leaned into me a little. "Let him go. He'll be fine if he's right beside me. I promise."

"We can't, ma'am. Standard orders when dealing with the bigger boys," one of the guards said.

"Right," I said, "because standard orders in regards to Nevermores are so set in stone, having been around for years." I let out a sigh and looked to Clark. He shook his head.

"They can't let him go until he's within his next confinement. That's the safest way to do this."

There was no use for it. At least they weren't beating him.

"Now what?" one of the other guards asked.

I stepped up to the fence while I broke up the remainder of the loaf of bread. Nevermores watched me closely, and one from the back more so than the rest. He was a large male . . . but both his feet were missing. His eyes narrowed as he stared at me, like he was weighing me. I shook my head and threw three-quarters of the loaf of bread over the top, away from the door into the range. The Nevermores inside the fence line froze in place as a unit, their noses lifted to the wind in tandem while the rain ran down over their yellowed skin. Then they broke from their paralysis and scrambled over one another as they fought to get to the chunks of bread. Mass hysteria broke out, fists and feet flying, and the pack let loose with their un-earthly howling and screeching.

From there the scene *seemed* to go downhill, but that was what I had counted on. I fed Sebastian a piece of stale bread as we sat on the wet ground, handing it to him in chunks. It was awkward with the catchpoles, but we made it work.

"Vincent wanted Bastian in right away," Clark said.

"I know. But I want a chance to actually make this work. Don't you?" I looked at him and he gave a nod.

The rain poured down around us, and the first pair of males squared off. This was going better than I had hoped.

I put my money on the larger of the two Nevermores. His body was tightly coiled with heavy muscles and he outweighed the smaller male by at least fifty pounds. They circled around one another, jabbing and growling as they tested the other's reach and fighting ability.

In a sudden flurry, they launched at one another, screaming their rage. The fight lasted maybe a whole minute, with a surprise victory to the smaller of the two men. He stood over his opponent and crowed to the cloud-ridden skies before he dropped and ripped the bigger man's throat out, sealing his win in blood. A ripple of chills went through me and I tucked my body tighter against Sebastian's. The soldiers around us didn't make a move, not even a gasp. I wondered how many times they'd seen this sort of thing.

From the back of the pack, the male with the miss-ing feet gave a soft grunt.

Next.

The word floated through my mind with an image of a young male. I shook my head. Imagining things again. I couldn't afford to let my mind wander like that.

The winner was immediately challenged by a younger male who looked a lot like the version I'd seen in my head only moments before. He was tall and lean, almost as tall as Sebastian, with a shock of red hair that stood on end as if he'd been electrocuted. Living here with Vincent, the possibility of that kind of torture was all too real. I had to work at putting away my sympathy for the red-headed male. He could be the one Sebastian faced later.

This second fight lasted longer. The two combatants wrestled to the ground, and mud covered their bodies in seconds. It was hard to follow the progress of the fight because of the dirt and the bodies of the other Nevermores darting around them, cheering them on. I'd catch a glimpse of an arm or leg, a flash of the red hair, and then nothing but a mass of Nevermore bodies.

"Get out of the way!" one of the soldiers yelled.

Clark looked at me. "Can you make them move?"

I wasn't sure, and I was afraid to try and fail. "Not right now, not when they haven't fully accepted me yet."

I looked away from him and back to the two contestants. I had no idea who was winning. The end came with a sudden loud crack followed by a scream. The fight was over, and this time the red-headed young one was the victor. He strutted around the compound and kicked at the limp body of his opponent as he passed, while he eyed up the rest of the pack. No one lifted their eyes to his, giving him the submission he was demanding with only his presence. He had no other challengers.

This was it.

"Now, we can put Sebastian in." I pulled the knife from my waist and cut the ropes from his wrist and neck before Clark or anyone else had time to protest. I bent and he lifted a foot while I sliced through that rope too.

There was a moment of stunned silence from the soldiers and then a steady clicking of guns being raised and safeties being flicked off.

"Mara, if he attacks, we'll be forced to shoot him." Clark's voice was dead even. I ignored him.

"Sebastian." I held my husband's head and pulled his face close to mine. "I need you to go in and take over the pack. We need them to help get us out of here, okay?" I kissed his lips and he nodded once and managed to wink at me, almost like the man he had been. "Missy, sit. Stay." I pointed and she slammed her butt onto the wet grass.

I turned my back to Sebastian and walked forward. He followed me to the gate where the nearest soldier opened the door and stood behind it, his eyes wide and full of fear.

"You are one crazy bitch," the soldier muttered.

"Love will do that to you," I said with a twist of

my lips. Sebastian stepped into the rifle range, the movement drawing all the Nevermores' eyes to him.

"Scout," I said. He jumped and I pointed in. Slinking along, he did as he was told and the Nevermores saw him listen. They saw him obey a human woman.

Before I could take another breath, the fight was on. The young buck rushed Sebastian and, without realizing it, me too. I started backward, reaching for the door.

The soldier slammed the gate shut with a rattle.

There was only one problem; he didn't wait until I was out of the way, and the door hammered my back and threw me further into the rifle range with the Nevermores and the raging male as he attacked Sebastian.

CHAPTER
TWENTY – ONE

Sebastian

I had no time to think about anything but the young Alpha coming at me. He was fast, and while winded from his first fight, his temper was hot.

There was yelling from the humans on the other side of the fence but I paid no attention to it.

Now was the time to fight or be killed. I focused on the male in front of me and swung a clawed hand at his face.

CHAPTER
TWENTY – TWO

Mara

"Get her out of there!" Clark snarled. The gate started to open, but then slammed shut a second time as the rest of the Nevermores surrounded me and Scout. They were too close to the gate, and the soldiers weren't taking any chances. Missy howled and threw herself at the fence.

"No! Sit, stay!" I locked eyes with her and she did as she was told, though her whole body trembled. I brushed the moisture from my face.

I couldn't really blame the soldiers. After all, not only had this been the ultimate goal, to put me in here, but the Nevermores had pretty much rushed the gate where I stood. They sniffed the air, particularly around my crotch, before they reached out to touch me and Scout with cautious fingers.

Sebastian already battled it out with the young male. He'd not noticed I was in the rifle range with him.

I stood slowly, while my heart hammered at breakneck speed. Scout stayed at my heels and pressed himself against me, looking to me for leadership in this new pack. Shit. This was not how I'd planned things to go.

I still had a few chunks of bread and I broke them up further. A woman made a grab for what I had and I slapped her hand down and growled at her, doing my best imitation of Sebastian and Scout. "No!"

She lowered her eyes and withdrew her hand.

I split the piece into four and slipped the first to Scout, who took it eagerly. Maybe if I showed him favoritism that might bring him up in the pack. Then I handed a piece to the woman who'd reached out. Her eyes filled with a joy so intense, it brought a lump to my throat. They were starving, doing their best to live, to exist. Though they weren't human as they had been, they still felt emotions, needs, and wants. The third piece I handed to a grizzled old male who looked like he'd been in his share of battles. I looked over my shoulder to see Sebastian pounding the living piss out of the young buck.

The last chunk went to Clark's ex-wife. Then I broke my last two chunks into as many pieces as I could, handing them out to the rest of the pack.

They took them eagerly, and when I growled and shooed them with my hands, they backed off. Maybe it was a good thing I was shoved in here. They weren't attacking me, and they were seeing me as the Alpha's mate, higher than them in pack standing. Maybe this would work after all.

A roar erupted from the fighting, and I turned to see Sebastian standing over the young buck, his foot on the throat of his opponent. The set of Bastian's shoulders, the tensing of his muscles . . . he was going to kill the other male. Before I thought better of it, I ran to them, pushing my way through the pack. They gave before me, letting me through. I stumbled, all but falling against Sebastian. I gripped his arm hard; his skin below my fingers was hot and flushed with adrenaline and blood lust.

"Don't kill him, Sebastian. You don't need to. He can help us."

I wasn't so sure I'd made the right move when Sebastian turned his eyes to me. Rage and a feral hunger flickered through them like flashes of lightning. I swallowed hard and put my other hand on his chest. "Come back to me, Bastian. You aren't a killer."

He shook his head slowly, sending a spray of water and blood off his head. The tension drained from him second by second. I held my breath until he lifted his foot and Buck, as I was already thinking of him, scrambled away with a groan.

Sebastian blinked several times and looked around. His eyes went from me to the pack and then to the gate. I wasn't supposed to be in here with him, not yet.

He clamped his hands on my shoulders and tugged me tightly against his body with a hard jerk. I clung to his arm as he circled it around my upper chest. He drew a breath and let out another roar. The pack cowered and bowed their heads one by one.

The message was clear even to me. He was the Alpha. I was his mate.

A voice shattered the moment. "Well, your methods seem to be working. You can stay with them then. I think you should be perfectly safe with your *Bastian* looking out for you."

I turned in Bastian's arms. Vincent stood at the doorway into the rifle range staring in at us. His hand was on a lock that hadn't been there before. His face was blank, but there was a tiny corner of a pink journal peeking out of his shirt collar.

So here it was, my punishment for reading the journal. I shouldn't have been surprised.

A crash of thunder made me flinch. The boom was followed by a brilliant bolt of lightning and a second round of thunder that made the pack around us cower. A summer storm was nothing to sneeze at, not here. The rain and wind would pick up and hypothermia was a distinct possibility in the West Coast climate. Already, gooseflesh popped up all over my arms in response to the dropping temperature.

I looked for Green through the crowd of soldiers. He held Missy's collar. "Green, watch over her."

He nodded and tugged Missy back a bit. She whined and lunged to get to me, and my throat tightened. A more loyal dog I had never met.

Sebastian pulled me tightly to his side and we

made our way toward the back of the rifle range. There was a hump in the ground used to deflect the missed bullets. As far as cover went, it was the only windbreak we had. The rest of the Nevermores circled in close as we sat. Their body heat radiated, surprising me. I glanced at Bastian and he was watching the others carefully. Every once in a while, one of the other Nevermores would glance my way and narrow their eyes and Bastian would snap a hand out and smack them.

So. Maybe I wasn't so accepted yet.

Still, the pack put something of a protective shield around us, using their bodies to help keep us warm. I curled against Bastian's side and let out a sigh. Something bumped into my hand and I looked down to see Buck pushing his fire-engine-red head up into my fingers. Sebastian growled at him, but I gave him a squeeze. "He wants comfort, not sex."

Bastian grunted, but didn't growl again. Buck let out a sigh as I smoothed his hair back.

I watched the soldiers watching us. Vincent raised his hand and waved it in a slow circle. "Back to the barracks. We'll see if she is still in love with her man in the morning."

The soldiers peeled away, all except Clark. He stood at the gate, a look of absolute horror etched into his face.

"Mara, I don't want to leave you in there. It's not safe." He glanced over his shoulder as Vincent stepped into the bunker. "He put a lock on that only he has the key for. I can't get you out."

I smiled at him and stroked Buck's hair while I leaned against Sebastian.

"Clark, in case we don't get a chance to see each other again, I want to thank you. You've been a good friend to me. I think you're a good man; don't let them turn you into anything else. And make sure Green takes care of Missy."

Clark's lips pressed into a thin line, and even with the distance between us, I could see the indecision warring in his eyes. He could shoot the lock off, but then all the Nevermores would be loose along with me.

"I'll be okay. I've got Sebastian, and apparently, a new family. If I know nothing else, I know the packs look out for one another, and for the moment, I'm one of them." I said the words to comfort him. But I realized what I was saying was true. I was probably safer out here in the rifle range than inside with Vincent.

And what no one seemed to have noticed was that I still had my knife. In all the scuffle, none of the soldiers had taken it from me.

"I'll check on you as often as I can."

Lightning flashed at the same time a crash of thunder erupted. They happened so close together, it was hard to say which one was first. The storm was on us.

Clark walked away as the rain poured down and the sky darkened. The brief flashes of lightning outlined the faces around me in sharp relief. I sat in the middle of a Nevermore pack, a place that should have me well and truly terrified. And yet, for the first time in weeks, I knew I was safe.

At least, I thought I was.

CHAPTER TWENTY – THREE

Sebastian

ear rocked through me with every breath I took. Mara was in far more danger than she realized, and I knew that if I was not totally vigilant, I would lose her to one of the pack.

The old Alpha pulled himself along the ground so he was at the edge of the huddle. His eyes met mine and he shook his head slowly.

You should not have claimed her. The other females will challenge her for the right to mate with you.

It was as if his images unleashed the females. Two of them snatched Mara from my side in a flash, and the bigger of the two threw her out into the open away from the pack. She hit the ground, slid, and was on her feet far faster than I had expected.

I leapt to my feet and let out a snarl at the female who circled her.

"No, Bastian. I will deal with this." Her voice was so calm, I wasn't sure I was hearing her right.

I turned to see her hand out to me, not to call me to her, but to stop me. There was no way she could survive this. I took a step and she snapped at me.

"I said, I would deal with this!"

I froze, torn between protecting her and understanding that if she did this, if she fought this female, the pack would truly be hers to command.

It took all my strength to nod and not tackle the female Nevermore to the ground. Mara circled with the female and the storm picked up its pace around us. There were no soldiers to cheer or call, there was nothing but the sound of the wind and the images that flooded my brain.

Scout slipped up beside me and I glanced at him. *She's strong enough. Strong female for strong Alpha.* The image was clear from him. He believed in Mara.

The female Nevermore let out a screech and threw her head backward, flexing her body. Mara took the opening and shot forward, her hand moving in a quick slashing movement.

A gasp ripped from the female, and I stared at the line of blood that bloomed across her bare belly. Not a deep wound, but a wound nonetheless.

"Come on, then, if you think you can take me." Mara beckoned to the female and while my eyes bugged out, my pride did a little back flip of joy. My mate was not weak, though she seemed soft.

The female leapt forward and they tumbled to the ground. Mara rolled with her and ended up on top. She pressed a knife to the female's throat, cutting in. "Live or die?"

The female squirmed and then went still. Mara stared down at her. "I know you understand me. Live?"

The female lifted both hands, palms to the sky. Mara got off her and then held out a hand to help her up. The female took it and launched at Mara, teeth bared.

I bolted forward, but wasn't fast enough to stop the female from slamming into Mara. This time, though, they didn't tumble. Mara held her ground, and drove her knife up and into the heart of the female. She died easily; there was nothing but surprise on her face as she slid to the ground at Mara's feet.

A flash of lightning snaked behind her, and for a moment, I wasn't sure she wasn't as wild as the rest of the Nevermores. Her eyes were wide and her skin splattered with mud and rain, and the scent of blood filled the air.

Shaking, soaked to the skin, Mara turned to me. Her eyes filled with tears as she shook her head slowly. "I didn't want to."

An image slammed into my brain, powerful and full of emotion. Regret and pain of an unnecessary death. The pack let out a low moan of understanding as the image floated through to them all, and several of them scooted forward, carefully ducking their heads in submission to Mara. One female, the pregnant one, took her hand and led her back to the rest of the pack. One by one they touched her, marked her as one of their own.

I waited for Mara to come to me as was my right as the Alpha, though I wanted nothing more than to scoop her up and hold her tightly.

She reached me and I took both hands, and once more, we settled into the huddle that would keep us warm through the night. Her head tucked into my shoulder and hot tears slid down my skin. I wrapped my arms around her and the pack curled in closer.

Mara may not have wanted to kill the female, and while that alone would have cemented her place, it was her regret that had made the transition easy. I lifted my head to the old Alpha when he gave a low grunt.

She is strong enough..

CHAPTER
TWENTY – FOUR

Mara

The fight left me physically and emotionally exhausted. Even with the rain hammering down, I slept.

The two of us were in the center of the pack. Scout was kind of curled around our legs and the rest of the members were snuggled up as close as they could be. Not only to conserve warmth, but I think to feel secure and safe. That was what I got from it. From the need to touch each other, and even to touch me after the fight. To acknowledge that they were safe with each other, and now with me too.

Sometime near morning, the storm broke. I only noticed because Scout shifted on our legs and I adjusted my position on the hard ground.

We woke to the rattle of the gate and a holler.

"Mara, I don't want you to have to fight for your food."

I scrambled to my feet, my heart beating hard at the sudden waking. My body was stiff and sore from sleeping on the ground and images of the fight from the night before flickered and danced in front of my eyes.

I swallowed hard and fought the fear that tried to curl through me. I had to be strong.

Across from me, Green stood with a basket of food on his hip and Missy at his side. She gave a bark as she saw me and jumped up, putting her front feet on the fence.

I thought of the moldy bread I'd given to Scout and was ashamed that I thought it was okay to feed it to him. Of course he'd eat it, he was starving. It didn't matter that the hunger was drug-induced.

Now, here I was about to get the same treatment as the Nevermores, despite the fact that I was still human. I let out a sigh, scrubbed my nose and walked to where Green stood. None of the Nevermores followed me.

He had a key for the new lock and he fumbled with it while I waited.

He opened the gate and thrust the basket of food through.

I stared into the basket of not-moldy bread, two plastic containers—one with beans, the other full of creamed corn—and a big plastic jug of water. "How did you get so much stuff?" I couldn't believe that Vincent would allow this much food to go to the Nevermores.

Green handed me a plastic glass. "Here. Don't share this with them; they'll drink from the puddles."

I took it and shook my head. "I know they're wild, but if they were your family, would you expect them to drink muddy rain water?"

Missy strained against the leash he had on her; I juggled the basket in order to reach a hand out to her. I managed to get a hand on her head and give her a quick rub before the barracks door behind Green opened.

"Shut the gate, kid!" a solider I didn't recognize yelled.

Green ducked his head, but not before I saw the high spots of shame on his cheeks. He shut the gate but didn't slide the lock into place. "No, I wouldn't want that, but I also know that if given the chance, they would tear me limb from limb. Even your Sebastian, given the right circumstance."

I stared at him, knowing that what he said was true. They would kill any human they could for food. My integration into the pack was nothing short of a miracle. A series of events that turned out even better than I had hoped.

Green leaned toward me, opened the gate and tucked a handgun into the waist of my jeans. "Clark asked me to give this to you. Just in case. If Sebastian turns on you, or stops protecting you, then you're going to need this. Here's the safety, just flick it off and you're good to go. It has five bullets in it."

I looked down and stared at the weapon tucked into my jeans. "I can't shoot him."

"You could wound him, though, to get away. And we'll hear the shots and come running." His eyes stared into mine.

I sighed. I couldn't explain how I knew I was safe. And it was no longer just Sebastian who would protect me, but the rest of the pack, too.

"I know you mean well, and I thank you for your concern, but it won't be necessary. Sebastian will take care of me." Still, I kept the gun. Because I was not so idiotic as to believe I wouldn't need it. There would be a time for sure. Only I was betting it wouldn't be a Nevermore that made me pull the trigger.

I turned and walked back to the pack that'd watched the entire exchange but hadn't approached.

I held the basket up, thinking about how they were going to love to eat what was in it. Before I could even say 'food', the pack swarmed around me. Laughing to myself at their ability to almost read my mind, I doled out the food. I kept the largest amount for myself and Sebastian, of course, but the rest I divided up as evenly as possible. Some of the pack was working on stripping the flesh off the two Nevermores that had died the day before. I did my best not to think about how they'd died. That I'd killed one of them and felt her blood run down my wrist.

I gave Bastian the whole container of beans as my stomach rolled with nausea. Nothing was going in my mouth anytime soon.

With one piece of bread left in my hand, I looked around for a Nevermore to give it to. Most were busy working on one of the bodies. I turned away from them to see Clark's ex-wife lying with her back to us. Ripples ran through her body as she shuddered so hard, the ground underneath her shifted. I turned to go to her. Sebastian put a hand on my arm and stopped me.

"Careful," he murmured softly.

I glanced over my shoulder at him and smiled, though it was hard to make my lips move that way. Nothing had gone the way I'd hoped other than the fact I hadn't been torn apart by the Nevermores. And now it looked like it was going to go even further downhill.

"Something's wrong with . . . Momma," I gave her a name impulsively, seeing as neither Clark nor Green had told me her name.

He nodded and let go. I made my way to Momma's side.

I bent down and touched her hip gently. Her skin was hot, burning up, but she was still shivering. She flinched as my skin came in contact with hers, and she curled up tighter against the blows I think she expected.

"Shhh. It's okay." I moved up around the side of her so I was in front of her and she could see me easily. She rolled her eyes up and I smiled down at her. "Come on, now, sit up and eat." I held out my hands and she reluctantly put hers in mine. Or at least, I thought it was reluctance. I helped her sit up, but it was quite the task. She was huge with her pregnancy, and her body shuddered over and over. A low moan slipped past her lips as she shifted her bulk.

I pressed the bread into her hands and she stared at me, tears slipping past her long eyelashes. A Nevermore crying was not something I would have ever thought to see.

I rubbed her shoulder. "Eat, you need to for the baby."

The life in her eyes, the gratitude that hovered there as she took the bread from me was clear as the sky above us. And it made me uncomfortable.

My first reaction to the Nevermores who'd surrounded our property had been to suggest just getting in the car and running them over in order to get away. But no matter that they were dangerous, they were in their own way sympathetic.

Momma ate the bread slowly between low moans, her body shivering. I kept a hand on her shoulder, steadying her. I was afraid I knew what was happening, but I wanted to be wrong. Please let me be wrong.

She took the bread, swallowed it down, and a split second later let out a keening wail that set the whole pack off. They howled with her, and she clutched at her belly.

There was a splash, and a clear liquid pooled out around her.

That was what I'd been afraid of. "Shit."

I helped Momma lie back while she moaned and clutched at her belly between convulsions. I waved at Sebastian. "She's having the baby!"

Bastian strode to my side and dropped into a crouch. I kept a hand on Momma and she clutched at me, fear written all over her face.

On impulse, I spun and yelled toward the barracks. "Green! Green! I need your help!"

But of course, there was no one up here. Really, what was I thinking, that they would hear me back in the bunker? Even if I fired the gun, I didn't think they would hear me that far underground despite what Green had said.

The other pack members crept closer, sniffing the air. Blood and amniotic fluid continued to flow in a steady drip from Momma. I shooed away the pack members. "Go on. She doesn't need you, right now."

If one of them so much as took a single sip of the muddy fluids, I would throw up on their heads.

Though I'd read a lot of books in preparation for being a mom myself, I'd never thought I'd be helping someone else give birth. Certainly not in an army camp's rifle range with no cover, no medical supplies, without even a bit of water to wash up.

I knew walking was good to move things along, so that was the first objective. "Sebastian, help me get her up." I tucked myself under one of her arms. Sebastian reached for her and she grabbed his forearms, her fingers digging into his muscle. His face tightened.

I tapped his other arm. "I mean it, help me get her up."

He took a deep breath and helped me get her on her feet. She moaned and wobbled, then tried to lie back down.

"No, not yet. Walking first." I tugged on her arm, encouraging her to step out with me. She took one step, then another, and soon we were slowly making our way around the perimeter of the range. With each step, her breathing improved and her face relaxed between contractions.

When a contraction would take her, she would pause and bend over, breathing through it carefully, giving me her weight. The spasm would pass and then we would keep going.

I made soothing noises, did what I could to encourage her. Occasionally, I touched her belly to feel the muscles contract. To me the contractions were coming not only closer together, but lasting longer too.

"You're getting close, I think."

Sebastian watched all of this from a distance with a very strange look on his face, one I couldn't identify and was too busy to analyze. When the other members of the pack tried to approach me and Momma he growled at them. They backed off and let the two of us have our space.

We walked for an hour and I could see Momma was getting tired. I took her back to the dirt berm that we'd slept against.

"Not the Hilton, but it will have to do." I found a relatively clean, dry spot for her to lie down and helped her ease herself to the ground.

It was then that the contractions ramped up, coming so fast and hard that I was pressed to say when one ended and the next started. Her whole body would tense and the muscles across her stomach would ripple and harden.

I took a glance between her legs. I was no doctor,

but I was pretty sure what I saw was the crown of the baby's head.

Momma sat up, her hair plastered to her face with sweat as she bore down. I put my hands on her knees and gave her a nod.

"That's it. You can do it, Momma." I squeezed my hands over her knees as if that would help her along. "The baby's almost here, another push."

She leaned forward and grabbed under her thighs as she let out a wail, screaming along with a contraction. The baby's head and shoulder slid free; I got my hands under the head and cradled her.

"Another push!"

She groaned and bore down. The next push did it, and I guided the babe the rest of the way out as Momma collapsed back to the ground. There was one more contraction and the placenta came out right after the baby. Cradling the baby to my chest, I used an elastic band from my hair to tie off the umbilical cord. Hardly sanitary, but it was all I had.

The baby gave a soft wail as I cleaned out the mouth and did my best to wipe her face clear of the excess fluids.

"It's a girl!" I shouted as I brought the tiny angel child around to show to her mother. The little one let out another wail. I burst into tears as I held her. Because . . . this could be me in a few months. Scared and hoping that someone was there to help me give birth in the middle of nowhere.

I wasn't sure if seeing Momma do it gave me hope . . . or added to the anxiety.

Momma propped herself up on her elbows and took me and the baby in with a single glance. Her eyelids fluttered and a low moan slipped from her as she reached for the baby. I started to hand her over and then stopped.

Momma's eyes narrowed and her tongue slid over her lips.

So hungry.

The thought hit me and I scrambled backward, holding the wailing child to my chest.

I glanced again at the child in my arms. The baby was definitely human.

I wanted to believe that the intensity I saw in Momma's eyes was that of a mother wanting to hold her firstborn.

But I could not deny what I was seeing happen right in front of me.

The child was a meal.

I remembered all too clearly telling Jessica that Nevermores would eat their own young if they came out as human, without the Nevermore genes.

Momma's fingertips brushed the baby girl as she lunged at us. A look of pure lusting hunger flashed over her face.

The drug was so powerful, the feral nature in her so intense that even her own child wouldn't be spared its wrath.

I'd wanted to believe that what was human inside Momma would override the animal instinct to eat another species' helpless newborn. But as she and the other Nevermores crept toward me with their mouths open and teeth snapping at the crying baby girl, I had to accept this for what it was.

A complete and utter disaster.

CHAPTER
TWENTY – FIVE

Sebastian

All the pack saw in Mara's arms was a different kind of food. One that was soft and full of life, one that would feed them for a day. I closed my eyes, wishing I could unsee the images that flickered through my mind. The feeling of teeth tearing into flesh, of gulping down tiny pieces of . . .

Is this what would happen when Mara gave birth?

Of course it was. Our child would be like this one, feeble and helpless, dependent on us to protect him or her.

My jaw twitched as I realized there was no safe place, no refuge we could make to protect a child.

Unless we made it for us now.

I strode forward, determined to make the pack leave the child.

CHAPTER TWENTY - SIX

Mara

I jumped clear of Momma's snarling reach and growled back at her. The baby wailed as I held her tightly. Already her tiny body shivered against the cool air on her fresh new skin.

What the hell was I going to do? I couldn't keep the child here in the rifle range. I had nothing to wrap her in, no breast milk or formula, and I wasn't entirely sure I could keep her safe from the whole pack, even with my new status. All it would take was one lapse on my count and she would be snatched from my arms.

A hand touched my shoulder and I spun with a gasp.

Sebastian stood behind me, a hard look etched into his face.

I stared up at him, tears streaming from my eyes. "Momma wants to eat her baby."

He nodded once. "I know."

He placed one big hand over the still-slick skin of the newborn. His big hand covered her entire torso, and the yellow skin against the brilliant pink of the baby girl was yet another contrast. Sebastian stared at the child, then slowly lifted his hand and pressed it against my belly. His understanding of the situation, and how very bad it was, went straight through me like a blade. How could I have ever doubted him?

"We have to get her out of here." I rocked her, doing my best to soothe her. "She isn't safe."

Sebastian nodded, bent and kissed the crook of my neck, going so far as to give me a soft nuzzle. Again, marking me as his mate and under his protection. A not-so-subtle reminder to the rest of the pack.

I leaned into him and his body curled around both me and the little girl. For a moment, I just breathed him and the child in. For a moment, I could pretend we were safe.

A hand brushed against my leg, shattering my refuge.

Sebastian snarled at the one who dared to come too close and the Nevermore backed up so fast he tripped over himself. I added my glare to Sebastian's snarl and the male Nevermore dropped his head, lowering his eyes.

I jiggled the baby, and finally resorted to putting my pinky finger in her mouth to give her something to suckle. She latched on and quieted down in my arms, in the shadow of Sebastian's protection. I knew it wouldn't last, though. She was hungry, and far too cold.

She needed a miracle if she was going to survive.

The creak of the bunker door opening brought all our heads around. I looked past Sebastian and my heart leapt.

There stood Green at the gate like an angel come from heaven to rescue the baby.

"Supper, Mara."

Was it that late already? I'd barely noticed the passage of time with Momma's labor, but a quick glance at the sky told me that indeed it was late in the day.

"I have to give her to him. He's her only chance," I said as much to convince myself as anyone else. I couldn't keep the baby alive. Her only hope was inside that bunker.

Sebastian gave me a gentle push and I walked to Green. The kid's eyes widened and his jaw dropped open as I drew close.

"Holy crap, the pregnant one didn't eat her baby?"

I frowned as horror spread through me at a slow, awful pace. "What do you mean? Was there . . . another pregnant Nevermore?"

Green nodded as he fumbled with the lock and finally opened the gate a few inches. Behind him at the bunker door two soldiers waited with their guns cocked. Apparently they didn't trust Green not to let me out.

He glanced back and nodded before he went on. "Three weeks ago another of the females gave birth; I think it was that one there." He pointed to a heavy-breasted brunette, and I could see she did indeed have some extra flesh around her middle. Not much, but more than any of the others.

"The baby came out, and before we could get in the cell, she'd grabbed it and taken a bite out of it. We wrestled her to the ground and took the kid, but . . . he didn't survive an hour."

The revulsion and horror that had been slowly growing in me took a distinct spike. How? How could a mother do that?

I cleared my throat, doing my best to smooth away that tremor I knew would be there. "Well, you've got chance number two, now." I stepped close to him and tried to transfer the baby into his arms.

He shook his head. "You don't understand. She won't be any better off with us, Mara. Can't you feed her?" He stared at me, and for a second his eyes dipped to my breasts with a blush. I stared back.

"She *won't* survive out here. I have nothing to wrap her in. She's already losing body heat, and I'm pretty sure I can't feed her. Just because I have boobs does not mean I can automatically produce milk on command," I half-hissed, half-whispered to him. Absolute and complete horror filled my heart where hope had only moments before resided. Green handed me the basket of food.

"I'll get you some blankets and more food for you. But you can't share it with the rest of them. I'm telling you that Vincent . . ." he glanced over his shoulder, "won't care if the baby lives or dies. It's just another mouth as far as he's concerned."

"Then tell Clark. This is his child."

"He doesn't think it is." Green shook his head. "I'm not trying to not help, Mara. But . . . the baby might be better off if it didn't survive. At least in this place."

If I'd had a free hand, I would have slapped him. He must have seen the intention in my face because he stepped back and shut the gate, locking it quickly.

I had no words as the lump in my throat grew, choking me. I'd helped to bring this baby girl into this world. I only hoped I hadn't done her a disservice.

"I'll bring up Vincent when I bring the blankets," Green said. "Maybe you can convince him."

"He won't help me or her." I tightened my arms around the little girl and she rooted against my chest, her tiny fists and face searching for her mother.

Green didn't answer me. What could he say?

My heart leapt when he unlocked the gate again. "Here, take this at least." He slipped off his jacket and handed it to me.

Then he shut the gate. The baby startled at the slam of the metal on metal and started to wail again. The pack rushed the fence, snarling and growling, as they reached for her. I pulled my knife from my belt and one-handed slashed at them. I caught several in the face and arms, but they were incensed, drawn by the cries and the smell of her brand-new body.

I kicked the food on the ground, scattering it.

They fell back. I may have been the Alpha's mate, but they were like sharks when the blood lust came over them.

Uncontrollable.

"There! You're hungry, go ahead and eat," I screamed at them as I kicked a loaf of bread high into the air. Their eyes traced it and they bolted after the food.

Momma watched me for a moment, then went with them, her body trailing the last of her placenta and umbilical cord.

I hurried across the rifle range to the farthest point of the compound. I tucked the knife through a belt loop and wrapped both me and the little girl in Green's jacket.

A glance over my shoulder showed Momma still with the rest of the pack, though her eyes kept coming back to me. She glared at me and I glared back.

"Bitch," I muttered under my breath. I wanted to hate her, but the logical part of me knew that hating her did not help the situation. I had to look at this as a survival of the fittest. And right now that meant that the little girl in my arms was in serious trouble.

As if my thoughts disturbed her, she squirmed in my arms and nuzzled at my chest again. A sigh slipped out of me. I didn't know if I had the milk to give her, but I had to try.

I slipped her under my shirt not only to protect her from the cool breeze, but I was able to hold her to my breast and attempt to get her to latch on. It wasn't easy—she couldn't seem to get it right and neither could I—but after several tries she latched on and started to suck. I gritted my teeth against the discomfort.

I had to hope that my swollen breasts would be able to give her some nourishment in time, that my milk would start with her suckling. It was the only hope she had.

"Love."

I looked up as Sebastian crouched down and slid over to me. I reached out for him with a free hand and pulled him in close. He whispered in my ear. "Love." His voice was rough and I wondered if his emotions were as torn up as mine. He wrapped his arms around the both of us, sheltering us again; his large hands rubbed my back as he consoled me.

Despite how the baby suckled, I could tell nothing was happening. I had no milk yet to give her. She gave a quiet mewl, then snuggled into my arms, falling into what I could only imagine was an exhausted sleep.

The tears started then, dripping down my face. No sobbing or any more screaming, just the steady flow of pain escaping me through each drip of a salty tear. This could be our child in a few short months. We could be fighting off a Nevermore pack just to keep our baby with us. And what if I didn't have milk for my own child? What would happen then?

I knew the answer, and my mind avoided the image that it tried to conjure.

I stroked the light blonde downy hair of the little girl that was still damp in patches. I wouldn't be able to sleep knowing how close the pack was. But if Sebastian claimed her too, maybe then she would be safe.

A short time passed in that quiet corner of the rifle range. A second commotion at the gate brought my head around. Sebastian stood and a low growl escaped him.

I stood and stared at the men approaching the gate. Green had come back with Vincent in tow. I made my way to the two of them, the baby still asleep in my arms. I had no doubt the lack of nourishment was already affecting her little body. She needed food, she needed warmth.

Green opened the gate. "You can come out now."

I didn't need urging. I hurried out, with only a single glance behind to Sebastian. He gave me a wink and I knew in my heart he understood. I had to protect this little girl. There was no other way.

Green closed the gate behind me, and I was outside the rifle range. I let out a sigh of relief, tension flowing from me. That was one danger crossed off the list. But I knew the baby was far from out of the woods yet.

Vincent snorted as he glanced to the bundle in my arms. "*This* is what you brought me up here for? You said it was a medical emergency. I assumed Mara had been injured."

With what looked like a casual flick of his hand, Vincent backhanded Green, knocking him to the ground.

"I don't like being lied to, Green."

"Sir, you said to bring you information of any changes, I thought—"

Vincent glared at him. "That is the problem. You thought. You are not here to think; you are here to do what I tell you to."

Green gave a curt nod and pushed to his feet. "Yes, sir." The mutinous look in his eyes, though, was good to see.

"Now, give me the baby," Vincent demanded, and held his hand out like he wanted a piece of fruit placed in it. Certainly not how you'd offer to hold a child.

I took a step back. "What are you going to do with her?" I held her tightly to me, my heart racing as I thought of the little girl that had belonged to Fran. The little girl that had gone "missing." The little girl no one saw inside the bunker.

I was not the blind innocent that Vincent thought. He was a rapist, and I had no doubt he had something to do with the other little girl's disappearance.

"I don't have to answer to you. Now give *it* to me," Vincent growled, as he reached for the little girl. I side-stepped him and kept him just out of reach.

My resolve hardened. Not mine by birth, the child was mine to protect, and I would do whatever it took. "She's *human,* Vincent. She isn't one of them. Look." I tried to hold her so he could see the pink skin and the pale blue eyes that blinked sleepily up at me.

"*It* will turn, just like the rest of them, and I'm not feeding any more monsters. Give *it* to me or I will take your Sebastian in *its* place," Vincent snarled as he lifted a handgun and pointed it into the range.

I cradled the babe and reached to my lower back where I'd put the gun Green had given to me. The gun he thought I would need against Sebastian and the pack. I took a few steps back, putting space between Vincent and me.

"Make your choice, woman." Vincent's hand didn't wobble as he held the gun steady.

"Green. Hold the baby for me." I handed the little girl to him before he could say no. He held her awkwardly and she squawked at the jiggling.

Carefully, I slipped the gun from my waistband as I faced Vincent. His eyes glittered with pure rage, and no small amount of madness.

A single slow breath in and I flicked the safety on the gun off. Vincent was only ten feet in front of me, there would be no missing. No recourse.

Letting the breath out, I pulled my hand from around my back, aimed, and fired at Vincent before Green saw what I was doing, before Vincent could do more than widen his eyes in surprise.

Before I could change my mind.

The trigger was easy to squeeze. It felt like the fake guns at the arcade. The recoil, though, was not so nice. I wasn't ready for the kick back, and it threw my arm up into the air, changing the trajectory of the bullet.

It hit Vincent in the throat, a bloom like a rose opening appearing on his bare skin. He fell over backward, his gun went off and the pack screamed. I didn't look to the pack, the image of Vincent held my attention. His hands scrabbled at his neck while he lay on the ground, and a gurgle of wet air hissed through the bullet-made tracheotomy.

The baby wailed. Shaking, I dropped the gun and held my arms out to Green. "Give her to me."

His eyes seemed to fill his entire blood-drained face. He handed her over, shaking. There were no soldiers at the top of the barracks as before. "Vincent didn't think he needed any guards?"

"I think he didn't want anyone to see what . . . I told him there was a baby. He knew. He made me out to be a liar."

I stared at him. His words only confirmed what I already thought. That Vincent had meant the child harm from the get-go. It wouldn't have mattered if she was a Nevermore baby or a human child.

"Mara, I can't believe you shot him . . ." Green stumbled over the words, not even getting a full sentence out.

"This is a dog-eat-dog world, Green. Vincent was going to kill her. We both know it. You just said it. And if he didn't kill her, he would have killed Sebastian and then killed her. I had the means to stop him." I cradled the squalling child to my chest. I needed a name for her. I couldn't just keep calling her "the baby."

My eyes refused to see the still-twitching body in front of us. Instead I turned and looked at the pack.

There on the ground was a Nevermore. His body was still, and already the pack was on him, taking bites out of his arms and legs. Not even dead yet, and they feasted.

Sebastian stood to one side, his eyes on me.

I turned my attention back to the child in my arms. I cooed to her, rocking her gently back and forth and slowly got her cries to ease. I didn't want to think about what had just happened. The previous deaths I'd caused had been reflexes, accidents, sheer defense. This was nothing of the sort. I'd planned it.

"What are we going to do, Mara?" Green asked.

I turned to him, frowning. "What do you mean?"

"About the body; we can't just leave it here. If the other men find out you shot Vincent, they'll kill you," he said. "Only a few of them are loyal to Clark."

I glanced over my shoulder to see the pack feasting on their own. Their cries were guttural, and at the same time I could almost *feel* the happiness radiating off them that they had food. Even the old Alpha with the missing feet had joined in.

Old Alpha . . . how did I know that?

I shook off the sensations flowing through me. I glanced at the barely dead and still-warm body of Vincent. My eyes went back to Sebastian. He still stood off to the side of the pack, letting them eat. I swallowed hard. Twice now I'd stopped him from killing and yet I'd killed three men, and the female Nevermore. Did it matter that I thought what I'd done was right? Did it make any difference in the end?

"The pack will eat him," I said.

A gust of air whooshed out of Green. "I was thinking the same thing. But . . . can you keep me safe while I drag his body in?" Green was already moving, picking up Vincent's legs. "Can you keep them away from the door, keep them off me?"

I nodded. I knew I could do that much. Besides, they were already busy, eating. Happy.

Content for the moment.

Green unlocked the gate and opened it. I stepped in first, but only a few of the pack noticed us. Those that did, crept forward, sniffing the air. I glanced away from them to where Vincent had died. There was a trail of blood from that spot into the rifle range.

"The other men are going to know. They can follow the blood and see that he was shot outside," I said, my voice monotone and strange, even to my own ears. There was no way we'd get away with this.

Green gave the body a last heave and the pack members who'd drawn close fell on it. The blood lust rolled over them, and they went wild with the fresh blood. While they would eat their own, they preferred not to, and it was only a flash before the entire pack had left their one meal to start in on Vincent.

"Hurry." I motioned for Green to go ahead of me. As I turned to step out, a pair of teeth snapped onto my calf. I screamed as teeth sliced into my flesh, and fingers gripped my upper leg.

With a roar, Sebastian leapt forward and smashed my assailant on the head. He knocked the Nevermore unconscious with that one blow.

I whimpered and put a hand to my leg while still holding the baby. The bite was an open gash. Green stepped close and put a hand under my arm to help me out of the cage. Sebastian, still riled up from the sudden attack, growled and tensed. I let go of Green and put a hand on Bastian's arm. "It's okay, love. Green is going to help me. I need his help, we both do if we're going to get out of here."

Sebastian stepped back, nodded and looked to Green. He gave a low grunt.

"Help her."

Green swallowed hard. "I'm trying."

The pack slipped in around Bastian, and dragged Vincent's body backward, farther into the rifle range. Bastian didn't move; he stared at me as Green helped me out and shut the gate. "I'll be back," I said. "You know that. I'm not leaving you."

He nodded and sat where he was, his back to the pack and their meal.

CHAPTER
TWENTY - SEVEN

Sebastian

Separated again. I knew it was the best for the baby, but I knew something Mara didn't. The child would not survive. That was why the mother tried to eat her. Not because she was human. I shook my head, frustrated that I couldn't explain that the child was sick, born with a defect in her body that wouldn't allow her to survive. That the female had been doing the only merciful thing she could.

The kid's words about the other female, the dark-haired Nevermore, came back to me. I turned and sent a message to the old Alpha.

Why did she, I tipped my head at the female in question, *bite her own child?*

The old Alpha lifted his head from where he feasted. *Can you not see that the one we eat was cruel? He was with her when she birthed. He hurt her and hurt the child. She protected the child the only way she could.*

Harsh reality slammed into me. The only way she could protect her child from Vincent was to kill him.

Your mate killed him. That is good. She is strong.

I grunted. *And yet she was repaid with a bite.*

The old Alpha shrugged. *Hunger drives us, you know that. And while she is strong, she still isn't us.*

I did know that. Even now, the pull to feast with them tore at my belly and my mind. I turned from them and scrounged through the range looking for anything that would fill my mouth, if not my belly.

A bush leaned in from the outside, loaded with thick blackberries. Most had been stripped, but the higher pieces of the bush were above where the other Nevermores could reach. I pulled them down and stuffed the berries into my mouth, savoring the burst of juices. Far from satisfying, it at least took my mind off what the rest of the pack did.

Of what they ate.

And the happiness that rolled off them as they devoured the bodies.

CHAPTER
TWENTY - EIGHT

Mara

"We'll tell them that one of the pack members jumped out, bit through Vincent's throat, and then dragged him into the rifle range," Green said as we slowly made our way to the bunker. I did my best not to listen to the happy chatter of the Nevermores as they ate.

I didn't glance back. "Will they believe that?"

He made a face. "Similar stuff has happened. You saw on the way here the guy that got dragged out of the truck, and those Nevermores are quick bastards. Vincent was cocky around them and it was getting worse. The more he tortured them, the more he treated them like they were just bad dogs that he could train."

As we came up to the bunker, Green stopped and faced me. "Clark will be in charge now."

Something about his voice slowed my feet. "That's good, we both know it is."

"For the men, yes. But for the baby? The thing is the baby's mom—that woman is Clark's ex-wife. He went back to find her once Vincent convinced him of a cure."

"You already told me that. Won't he be happy that I saved his daughter?" I asked, rocking the little girl in my arms as she fussed a little.

"Clark wasn't sure the baby was his. That's why he wouldn't come up here with Vincent. I tried to get him to, but he refused. I don't know that he won't want to throw the baby away . . ."

"It was better that he didn't come up seeing what happened," I said. "I can't believe he'd be as callous as Vincent, though. He's not like that."

Green nodded, but he hunched his shoulders like he wasn't sure.

Even though I said it would be fine, I knew convincing Clark to help me with the baby was not going to be easy. Green touched me on the shoulder. "How can you be sure the baby isn't one of them—that she's human?"

I stared down at the bundle I held. She was wrapped in Green's jacket with only her tiny face peeking out. Sound asleep and her body exhausted from lack of food and all the goings-on, she looked like a perfect angel with her soft pink skin and downy blond hair. "I don't think she is." I looked up at him, thinking of all the things I'd read about birth in the last few years, all the articles I'd devoured looking for help in my own situation. "Green, there are documented cases of women infected with AIDS that don't pass the disease on to their children. I think maybe something like that has happened here. Her skin is normal; she isn't trying to eat us. I would know, I stuck my nipple in her mouth." I smiled up at him, but he didn't smile back as I'd hoped.

The bunker opened up as he reached for the door, and Clark stepped out, his brown hair rumpled and his eyes rimmed in red as if he'd been crying. "What's taking so long?"

My heart softened; I knew the pain of losing all you held dear.

"Vincent was attacked and pulled into the range," I said.

His eyes went past us to the mob of Nevermores over the two bodies. "He was getting cocky."

Green nodded, a little too vigorously. "He managed to shoot one of them, but we couldn't help him."

I adjusted my stance so Clark had no choice but to look at me. His eyes dipped down to the tiny girl in my arms. I summoned up a smile. "She's all right; she's human." I limped toward him. He froze, his jaw trembling. There seemed to be a war in his eyes, but slowly his heart won out. He held out his arms and I placed her in them. She whimpered in her sleep and twisted her head toward him, almost as if she knew him.

"She needs a name," I said.

Clark didn't say anything at first. He just stared at his daughter with an intensity that only a new father could produce. Emotions flickered across his face: love, sadness, and a fierceness that could only be his desire to protect her.

He looked up at me. "I don't know if she's mine."

"She's yours, Clark. That is all there is to it," I said. She needed him, and I thought maybe he needed her just as much.

"She looks like an angel." He laughed a little. "Look at me going all soft."

I smiled, and then grimaced as my leg spasmed where I'd been bitten. "I thought the same thing."

Clark nodded and ran a finger over her cheek. She opened her eyes, blinking several times. His throat bobbed and he seemed to be struggling to speak.

"Seraphima . . . I think that would be a good name. It was my mother's name." Clark looked to me and I nodded.

"I think it's perfect for a little angel."

He turned and went back down into the bunker, ignoring me and Green, his attention solely on his girl.

I waited until he was out of earshot. "He didn't even ask if we were sure about Vincent. Shouldn't he want more details?"

Green shrugged. "I told you, men are killed all the time. We rarely ask questions when someone doesn't come back. I mean, why, when the answer is always the same as to how they died?"

He helped me into the bunker and we made our

way to a brightly lit area that I hadn't been in previously. It was clean with white walls and gleaming surfaces that highlighted the medical tools spread about.

"I don't know much about stitching wounds," Green said, as he helped me onto a chair. "But I think we should disinfect it and wrap it tightly."

I nodded and scooted up onto the table. I took a look around the room, noting the differences here than in the other parts of the gloomy bunker. It looked as though it was not only regularly cleaned, but that there was a great deal of power being used with the lights and equipment. I frowned when my gaze landed on the soldering gun. There were bits of plastic stuck to it. I leaned over and picked it up.

No, not plastic.

Charred flesh.

I all but threw the gun across the room. "What the hell is this place?"

Green shook his head as he prepared a tray of antiseptics and wraps.

"It's where Vincent worked on training the Nevermores. Torturing them, for the most part, like you said. He liked to burn them."

The new scars on Sebastian had a whole new meaning. "Sebastian?"

"Yeah, but Clark and I got him out as quickly as we could. It wasn't as bad as the others." He looked at me. "We were doing our best."

I put a hand on his shoulder. "Thank you." I shivered. "Gives this place a whole new feeling when you know that it wasn't used to heal, but to maim."

Green was quick with the cleanup and wrapping of my leg. I gritted my teeth through the worst of it which was mostly the iodine. My body relaxed as he finished up the last layer of the wrap. He stood and held a hand out to me. "See how that is."

I tested my weight on my leg. The wrap gave me a little support, so there was that.

"Thanks." I rubbed at the back of my neck. I was exhausted, the mental and physical strain of the last couple of days was finally catching up to me. "Where is Missy?"

"She's in your room. I keep her there and just take her out once in a while. Vincent . . . well, it doesn't matter now, but he was threatening her too."

My jaw ticked. I struggled to find any part of me that felt bad for shooting the asshole who was being eaten on the rifle range.

There was a knock on the door and we both turned. Clark stepped into the room. In his arms, Seraphima was wrapped in a fluffy pink blanket he'd found only God knew where. Worry creased his brow.

"Mara, I need you to feed her. She isn't taking anything from me." He handed her over to me along with a bottle.

"Where did you find this stuff?"

He shrugged. "The emergency supplies are simple, but they include a bit for babies, too."

"Is this formula?"

He nodded. "Yes."

Hope bloomed sudden and hot. "You need to eat, little one." I cradled her in my arms and stared down at her sweet little face, which was fading from the healthy pink of a newborn to a pale yellow.

I blinked, shocked at the sudden change in just the hour or so we'd been inside.

I sucked in a breath of air and looked up to see the concern on Clark's face. It wasn't her eating he was concerned about, it was the color of her skin.

Moving swiftly, I stripped her of her coverings and laid her out on one of the tables. Her body was indeed yellowing, but there was no hint of a marking like the broom flower, as the Nevermores carried.

"I think she's jaundiced." I looked up and caught Clark's eyes. "I think if we get her eating, that will flush her system." I struggled to recall all the books I'd read on early childcare. I put a hand to my head. "That's the only thing we can do."

I wrapped Seraphima back up and held her tightly, whispering to her. Clark stepped forward, everything about him vibrating with intensity. "Mara, I don't know how to help her. Please do something."

I took the bottle from him and shook it, checked the temperature of the formula on my wrist. "She needs to eat. That is all I know." I cradled her close and managed to get the bottle in her mouth. She took a few sucks and then a few more, but after less than an ounce she fell asleep. Exhausted.

"That's it, that's all she'll eat?" Clark breathed over my shoulder.

"I'm not a doctor, or even a nurse, I'm not entirely sure that there is anything else I can do." I rocked Seraphima as I fought to recall everything I'd read about issues babies could face after being born. "Isn't there anyone who has some medical training here?"

Both men went very still and I looked from one to the other. "What? Is there someone else?"

Green nodded slowly. "Donavan, he's a doctor. But he's crazy, gone over the deep end when his wife took the Nevermore shot. I mean . . . he is working on a cure, but I'm not sure I would trust him with a baby."

"I agree," Clark said. "I'm not willing to take the chance that he would hurt her. Even if it was an accident."

I stared at them both as the frustration grew. "Are you serious? If he's her only hope, then what? You just watch her die? What if she has an infection? He could have antibiotics!" Neither of them said anything so I tried a different tactic. "Do you have any idea what I would do to see my own child saved? What I would give up, who I would beg? Anyone. I would do *anything*." I stepped toward Clark. Seraphima's slow breathing and her very, very deep sleep was disconcerting. She should have been screaming bloody blue murder for more food, something she'd had only a few sips of since she'd been born.

"I'd do anything to save her," Clark snapped. I went toe to toe with him.

"Then talk with Donavan, beg him if you have to. We don't know what is wrong with her, and if we don't hurry, it will be too late. She's too young and weak to fight this off—whatever it is—on her own."

My throat closed at what I was saying, and I tucked my head down against Seraphima's to hide the tears.

Footsteps stomped away and when I looked up it was just me and Green again.

"He'll do right by her. This baby is all he's got left," Green said.

I nodded and crooned to the bundle in my arms. I could only hope Green was right.

Chapter Twenty – Nine

Sebastian

The bodies were devoured by the next morning, picked clean, and even some of the bones from the fingers and feet had been chewed off. No one had come out of the bunker since Mara had gone in.

It was as if the humans had forgotten us.

I crouched beside the old Alpha. *You will die when the pack outside the fence finds us.*

He nodded once. *Yes. But that is the way. The strong survive. Even now we are changing.* He lifted his hand and brought one finger after the other to his thumb. I'd already seen that was the case in my own hands. The numbing sensation faded, and my dexterity was coming back.

The pack, though, will strike soon. They can sense the weakness in the humans here. Even you must feel it.

Now it was my turn to nod. I did feel the lives of the men in the bunker coming to the end. But Mara was with them and I had to get her away first. In the open, I could protect her. Caged as I was, there was only so much I could do.

Why hadn't she come out?

Were they hurting her?

I reached for her mind as I'd done before. Straining myself, I was able to pick up a glimmer of her thoughts. Fear and sorrow, pain. She was hurting. I leapt to my feet and ran to the gate. Her mind became a tumult of emotion. Heart pain then, not physical pain. I closed my eyes and leaned my head against the fence.

I had no idea how I was going to get her away. I turned my head and looked back the way I'd come. From the far side of the fence, on the outside edge of the perimeter fence was something I'd been dreading. The eyes of the pack that gathered.

They shifted between the bushes and trees, their eyes on me.

While I didn't doubt my own abilities, I wouldn't just be fighting for myself. "Scout."

He lifted his head and the pack trembled, cowering at the sound of my voice. He scooted across the ground and I crouched down beside him. Casually I put an arm across his shoulders.

Those ones will hurt my mate if they get close to her. If something happens . . . you must protect her.

He tipped his head to one side. *Of course. Why wouldn't I? She's proven herself again and again to be an Alpha. Fed us. Protected us. Killed when she had to.*

I shouldn't have been surprised. I squeezed his shoulders and let him go with a quick push.

The tension in the air continued to grow as the other pack tested the fence over and over again. No one came out of the barracks to kill them or scare them away, and they grew bolder with each minute.

The time was coming when they would pounce.

And when they did I had to be ready.

Which was why it was with great surprise that I saw the one called Clark approach the fence on the second day.

"You love her?"

I blinked at him, then gave a quick nod.

"Then you know she will never be safe with you. She's caring for my daughter now." He pulled a key from his pocket and slid it into the lock. He opened the door and backed away. "Don't make me shoot you. I'm only letting you go because she cares about you. No other reason."

I just stared at him, and held a hand up to the pack as they crept forward. Was this some sort of trick? I wasn't sure I trusted him any more than Vincent.

"The front gate will be opened for you. Take your pack and go."

He turned and jogged back to the barracks. He opened the door and two men with long guns stepped out and climbed, high onto the top of the bunker.

Clark disappeared, and this was our chance. I gave a grunt and the pack followed me.

A part of me knew that Clark was right, this was my chance. But I knew Mara wouldn't leave without me.

Which meant I had to find a place to wait for her. I glanced to the side to where the other pack mimicked our pace. A place to wait for Mara was going to be much harder than it sounded.

CHAPTER THIRTY

$\mathcal{M}ara$

The next two days were nothing short of my own personal hell. I barely slept, hardly ate, and truly could do nothing but hold Seraphima close and pray she could fight this off—whatever it was that was wrong with her.

The small hope that Donavan could help was gone in a single attempt at contacting him.

"I won't help those who've done all they can to stop me from finding a cure," were his words over the CB radio, and then nothing but dead silence.

He didn't even give Clark the chance to tell him that it was a child's life that hung in the balance. Donavan, believing that Vincent was alive, refused to help us on those grounds alone.

I couldn't blame him after reading through Juliana's diary.

But it didn't change the fact that Seraphima was

slowly slipping away from us. She ate a little here and there; the formula, though, wasn't enough.

She slept more and more, her body listless. I woke her and tried to feed her every hour, but most times she refused the bottle, or took only a sip or two.

My heart begged her to live, to help me believe there was hope, that there were good things left in this world worth fighting for.

I prayed more than I ever had in my life, bargaining with God to let her live, to spare her life.

The days were a blur of hope and despair, of anger and grief. Through it all, Missy never left my side except when Green took her down to the dungeons to do her business. Otherwise, she was there, pressed against my leg, giving me her comfort the only way she could. Her big dark eyes were locked on the baby. More than once she nudged the tiny girl, as if she could encourage her to be strong.

To fight whatever it was that slowly took her closer to death.

We were losing Seraphima, moment by moment, and both Clark and I knew it. There were times I felt her heart falter, felt her breathing hitch as she struggled for one more breath. I began to doubt that even if Donavan had taken her in that he could have helped her.

Clark ranted and raved at Donavan, the world, and God, his shouts and anger not once disturbing the baby. I wanted to rant with him, but I knew it wouldn't help her.

Nothing would help her but a miracle that was not coming.

The morning of the third day, I startled awake. My arms were numb from holding Seraphima all night long. All I could do was hold her, and pray that my love for her was enough to keep her going. To get her through this.

I jiggled her softly and her head rolled. Her tiny lips were pale, and her chest was still. I stripped the blanket off her.

A sob caught in my throat as I listened with my ear pressed against her silent body. Missy whined and pawed at my leg. Agitated, she pushed her nose against the bottom of Seraphima's wrapped-up legs.

"Oh, please, no," I whispered as my fingertips brushed against her cold skin, but the reality had finally happened. She was gone. Tears streamed down my face and I held her to my chest, rocking her one last time. "Oh, baby girl, please don't leave us."

The door creaked open and Clark stepped in, his uniform rumpled, his eyes tired and drawn. We'd been sleeping in shifts. I wasn't sure if it would be better for him or worse that she'd died in my arms. I couldn't say the words. I couldn't tell him, but my tears were enough.

He knelt in front of me and I slipped Seraphima into his arms as if she were still alive and he cradled her the same way. As if she were still with us.

"I'm so sorry, baby girl," he whispered. "I'm so sorry." His shoulders began to shake and I did the only thing I could. I bent forward and wrapped my arms around him and held him as he grieved for his daughter. The grief was one I knew all too well, the loss of a child, the knowledge that you would never see them grow and learn, that you would never hold them tight. So much lost in that moment . . . so much potential, so much love.

We cried until the tears dried in streaks and the shudders racking us both subsided.

"We need to bury her." Clark stared into my face from only inches away. I blinked and took a slow breath as I nodded.

"Deep, it has to be deep so she will be safe."

He closed his eyes and a single tear escaped from under one.

We both knew that a shallow grave would be quickly unearthed by one type of animal or another.

He opened his eyes and leaned forward. He pressed his lips to mine, softly, carefully with no lust or craving behind it. "Thank you, for loving her. You were her angel when she needed you."

I bobbed my head, as the tears welled again. "Thank you for letting me."

There were no more words between us. He went and gathered men as I wrapped Seraphima in her pink blanket. I couldn't bear to cover her face, not yet. I kept an arm around her, and the other hand on the top of Missy's head.

That day was silent as the men went about digging a ten-foot hole on the back side of the bunker away from the rifle range. The men took turns with the shovel and straight bar. I didn't look at the rifle range as I sat waiting for the hole to be finished. The quiet of the day was only broken by a grunt here and there from one of the men. All of us had lost loved ones, but to see a man bury his baby daughter was a pain every soldier seemed to feel.

At the end of the day, as the sun began to set, we wrapped Seraphima in one more blanket and I finally had to force myself to cover her tiny face. "Goodnight, sweet girl," I whispered as Clark took her and jumped down into the hole with her. He bent over her, and though I couldn't hear the words, the pain in them as he spoke quietly to her was obvious. I looked away as Green approached. He held out a ratty old pink and purple teddy bear and offered it to Clark.

"She might need it." His eyes were glassy with unshed tears as he stepped back and ducked his head. The entire troupe was there, their eyes and hearts melting with the loss of a child who wasn't even their own, the grief of their friend bringing home perhaps the losses they'd all had over the last few months. All the burials they'd not been able to have, all the goodbyes they'd not had time to utter.

Clark filled the hole himself, not once letting any of his men take a turn on the shovel. I couldn't stay any longer, not without losing my composure again. I just wanted Sebastian, to feel his arms around me.

I was no longer a prisoner. Gripping the key to the lock on the rifle range, I made my way there. I hadn't seen Sebastian in the last three days as I fought for Seraphima's life, and my heart ached to be with him and to have him hold me.

The rifle range was strangely silent as I approached and my heart began to pound with fear instead of grief. The last ten feet I ran to the gate. "Sebastian!" I screamed.

There wasn't an answer. The door was unlocked, open.

I slipped through and ran inside. I spun in a circle looking for them. They weren't here, and I knew they weren't in the bunker. I let out a whistle, hoping Scout would hear me. I waited but there was no response. This was not happening.

"Sebastian!" I choked on his name as I struggled to understand. Where were they? Had Clark killed them? No, I had to believe he wouldn't do that. Not when he knew Sebastian still loved me.

"Clark let them go." Green's voice turned me around. "He didn't want to kill them. He knew about Sebastian and the scrawny one. So he let them go. He figured they'd have a better chance that way. The other men were talking about just shooting them all."

I slid to the ground, my body shaking so hard, my legs would no longer support me. "Sebastian wouldn't leave me."

Green shrugged and crouched down to my level. He frowned, and then looked toward the main entrance to the barracks. "He took off with the rest of them, the minute the gate was open. Maybe he finally lost himself to the drug." He paused. "I thought he was coming around too, but when he was offered the freedom he took it. I'd hoped he could be the one to help Donavan find the cure."

I dug my hands into the dirt as I struggled to breathe around the anxiety that coursed through me. I focused on the rocks under my hands, squeezed them until the pain helped to center me. "No. It's been too long. If Bastian was going to shift, if he was going to lose himself, it would have been before now."

Green held out a hand. "There's nothing we can do. He's gone. Come on, let's go back inside."

I sat there and closed my eyes, willing . . . I didn't know what I was willing to happen. I only knew Bastian wouldn't have left me.

Danger. The word came with an image of multiple Nevermores, ones I didn't recognize. I opened my eyes.

"He's trying to protect me."

An exasperated sigh slid out of Green. "Look, I get it, you want to believe he's not gone. We've all had that. I mean, you've had him with you longer than any of us got with our family members." Bitterness laced his words and I stared at him.

"It's not a competition. I don't win an award because he was with me longer, you know." I brushed away his hand and stood on my own. The men here didn't care about Sebastian. He was just another mouth to feed, another monster. Even Green, who I thought was on my side.

But I wasn't giving up on my husband. Not for a second.

Stomping my way into the bunker, I went to find Clark. He was in the war room with three other men. When he saw me, he waved them out. "We'll discuss this more tonight, boys. I want to be very sure it's possible before we attempt anything."

The other men left, nodding to me as they stepped out the door. It clicked softly behind them, leaving Clark and me alone.

"Mara, we're going to attack Donavan's in three days' time. I don't know what to do with you. I can't have you fighting, and I can't leave you behind." There was genuine concern in his voice and it slowed my anger, but only for a moment.

"Why did you let the pack go? You knew Sebastian still had a connection to me." I folded my arms over my chest and glared at him. A sudden urge to leap at him, to attack him caught me unawares. I struggled with the sensation, tightening my arms on myself. He didn't seem to notice.

Clark scrubbed his hands over his face, his short stubble rasping on his palms the only sound.

"I can't feed them, and they *were* starving. I know they'll eat anything, grass, leaves, sticks, bugs. But I couldn't watch Diana live like an animal any more. And I couldn't watch her let the other monsters ride her."

Ride her.

I slumped into the nearest chair, my heart freezing over. "Please tell me Sebastian wasn't one of the men who . . ." I couldn't even say it out loud.

Clark didn't move at first, and then slowly shook his head. "No, Sebastian never touched her, not as far as I know. I've had men watching, keeping an eye on them. The reported back that Bastian wasn't touching the other females, but the males were . . . mating with those females who were letting them."

I let out a breath that tried to turn into a sob. I bit it down, knowing it wouldn't help. Tears were useless in this world we lived in now. I covered my face with my hands and wiped my eyes clear. "He's still out there. He won't leave me."

Clark walked over to me and crouched, taking my hands in his. My jaw tightened. I knew he thought he was being kind, that he thought he was doing the right thing.

"I'm sorry this hurt you, Mara. But believe me, it's better this way. The pain will ease. I promise. I know firsthand, and the best thing I've done for Diana was to let her go completely. To stop trying to make her something she's not. She's not human anymore. She tried to eat . . ." He couldn't seem to finish that sentence. The pain of losing his daughter was still too raw. I didn't blame him for that.

I did, however, blame him for taking things a step too far. I wasn't interested in him that way, not in the least. For the moment, I'd pretend nothing happened.

He squeezed my fingers and then brushed a strand of hair from my face, his eyes never leaving mine. "You're a good woman, Mara, faithful, and kind, strong and a fighter all rolled into one person. A person I wish I'd met in another time."

"Don't do this, Clark. As far as I'm concerned, I'm still married." I tried to pull back, but the chair prevented me from doing anything but squirm.

His hands tightened on mine. "Tell me your heart isn't beating faster, that you don't want to be held by a man who won't turn on you, one that can keep you safe as well as love you and your child."

My throat started to ache and yes, my heart was beating faster, but it was from a strange mixture of fear and shame . . . and even sadness. What he was saying was true and not, at the same time. Because I wanted Sebastian, not Clark. I wanted my husband to hold me and our child, not another man. I had to get out of here. I had to find Sebastian.

He stared into my eyes and I did my best to give nothing back. I did not want to encourage what I was sure was only an infatuation because of the grief we shared over losing Seraphima. He cared for me because I'd tried so hard to save his girl. But I couldn't say that. I wasn't that cruel.

"I'm sorry, Clark, I can't. I love him and that won't change. Not ever." The words slid out of me, almost word for word the same as the dream I'd had where he'd held me back as Sebastian walked away. I hadn't even realized that I'd been repeating it until I'd spoken.

He surprised me by smiling. "It's okay, Mara. We've got a lot of time, and I think that's all you need." He lifted my hands and kissed the back of each one, then stood.

"I'm going after Sebastian." I pulled my hands back and tucked them into my pockets. "I'm not giving up on him."

Clark's smile slipped a little. "Let me show you what we've got here first. If you still want to leave, I won't stop you. But I think this might change your mind."

He tapped a single paper on the desk.

"The last report Vincent received was that Donavan was close to a breakthrough on finding a cure."

"Ha! I bet you're wishing you hadn't let Sebastian go now. He could have been the key to the cure."

Clark grunted, nonplussed by my snark. "Possibly. Or he could be a complete one-off. An anomaly that can't be duplicated which helps no one."

My brain finally caught up with what he was saying instead of trying to deflect his words. A cure. All that Vincent had been saying might be true after all? If there was truly a cure, I wanted it. I needed it for Sebastian, to bring him all the way back to me. A small spark of hope flared where for so long there had been nothing but day-to-day survival.

Clark continued, "I've got to find a way into that compound. If that cure is really happening, we need to be on hand for it. From what I understand, Donavan is no more stable than Vincent was. Less cruel perhaps, but no more stable." He stared at the paper. "If . . . if we can get this cure and start using it on the Nevermores, we can bring people back, Mara."

I arched an eyebrow. "I understand what a cure means."

He grinned, but it was a tired smile. "We need to take control of his compound so we can monitor what he's doing and how the cure is being used. I've no doubt that he can't mass produce it from where he is, but if we can get to him, then we can get the cure to people who are able to get that production happening."

I wasn't so sure that was a good idea, seeing as the last mass production drug had brought about Nevermores in the first place. I frowned. "Wait, what do you mean about getting the cure to other people who can produce the drug?"

He turned and pulled a few more sheets of paper off the shelf behind him. "There are other safe places, Mara. We aren't the only people left alive, you know. While there aren't that many," he shifted the paper, "they are out there. And they have facilities and power."

"Then why the hell aren't we going there?"

He glared at me. "What do you think I've been trying to do? Vincent was sent here to get to Donavan. To help get the cure to these people," he shook the paper again. "Vincent was so hell-bent on revenge, all he did was attack Donavan, which made him seal up his goddamn compound."

"Then why the hell do you think that attacking him will help this time?" I struggled not to yell at him. His reasoning was flawed.

"Because this time he's lost some of his key men. He had them out in the city, doing God only knows what. And they were killed. Five of his best shooters."

"You mean snipers, don't you?" I stared hard at him and he nodded.

He put the papers back onto the shelf. "I'm trying to help the world, Mara. Not just you, not just Diana or Sebastian. But the world. I need to get into that compound."

I thought he was being a tad bit melodramatic.

Why did he think that this Donavan was the only one who could be working on a cure? Surely there were other scientists in other places also attempting to find a way to reverse the Nevermore effect. For now, I was going to humor him. I mean, what other choice did I have? If there was a cure, I wanted it for Sebastian. And I would do whatever it took to get it for him.

Clark sat down across from me. "I'm thinking that perhaps a distraction will help us break through. Something that would keep Donavan's eyes on the front of his compound while we hit it from behind. Any thoughts?" He lifted an eyebrow at me and I frowned.

"What about a messenger?" I asked. Clark shook his head.

"No, it's been done. He just shoots the messengers now."

A soft knock on the door and we turned in tandem. Green stuck his head in.

"You said to come down here when I was finished."

Clark nodded and pointed to another chair.

"Have a seat. Mara and I were discussing a distraction for Donavan."

Green came in and Missy was with him. She wiggled her whole body when she saw me but quickly sat at my side, happy to just have my hand on her head.

I turned my attention back to Clark. "Clark, I know what Donavan did to Seraphima—turning his back on helping her—is horrible, but to waste more lives on revenge is . . . it's a waste. This world doesn't need more death."

Clark took a deep breath. "I'd be lying if I said it wasn't somewhat about revenge. But on top of the cure, he controls the harbor, the ships, and any chance we have of making it to the mainland. That is our destination. There are more people like us. All of that adds up to one thing. We need that compound. We need Donavan."

I frowned and rubbed at my cheek. "I still don't understand why would he be the one to find the cure? What makes him so special?"

Clark and Green both stared at me, eyes wide, but it was Clark who answered my question. "He developed Nevermore and used his wife as a test subject. She had cancer and had been told it was terminal. Mara . . . this is ground zero."

Chapter
Thirty - One

Sebastian

Outside the gates was the freedom the pack craved. They ran and I wanted to run. Wanted to feel the wind against my face and the smell of prey as it scattered ahead of us. But that wasn't for me anymore. I struggled against the call of the other Nevermores. Struggled against the desire for food and other things. One of the Nevermore females brushed up against my side.

I adjusted the old Alpha who I carried on my back.

You should leave me.

A part of me knew he was right. The other part knew that Mara would want me to do the right thing. To help him. I glanced over my shoulder at him.

They will kill you.

They will kill us both if you don't leave me.

His words were timed perfectly. The pack that had

been circling the barracks and dodging our heels as we ran caught up with us at the edge of a lake. Water so deep and wide there would be no crossing it, which meant we were driven down the pathways surrounding the edge.

Behind us came the howls and shrieks of the Nevermores as they hunted us. No, not us.

Me.

I was the Alpha. I was the one they wanted to attack, the one they wanted to prove they were stronger than. The only one not wanting it was the single female. I felt her mind brush against mine, but she could not protect me.

Either run faster or put me down.

I tightened my hold on his legs and sprinted forward. With a single image, I sent the pack around the lake. I veered to the side away from the lake which dropped into a steep descent riddled with loose rocks and small trees.

Half running, half sliding, I made it to the bottom of the ravine. I slid behind a downed log resting across a small creek, and dropped to my knees. The old Alpha dropped beside me and we peered over the log in the direction we'd come.

A few of the new Nevermores paused at the top of the path, sniffed the air, but then went after the main group.

You should not have left your pack.

I rolled my eyes. *Mara is my pack. I'm going back for her.*

That stopped him from speaking.

Leave me here.

I ignored him.

I waited until I was sure we would not be discovered before I picked him up. Tried to pick him up. He clawed and bit at me when I came close.

Leave me here. I am a burden. Go to your pack.

I crouched by him and frowned. I didn't want to leave him, but I knew he was right. He was a burden. I couldn't save him and Mara. I clapped a hand on his shoulder.

"Thank you."

He grunted. "Welcome."

My eyes widened and he smiled. *Perhaps we all will come back.*

I stood, not sure what to think or say to that.

I left him by the creek, thinking he would survive a little while on his own. Or at least until the pack found him and likely then he would die.

I hadn't gone far before I heard the bellow of a Nevermore male. They'd found the old Alpha then, far sooner than I thought. I froze, and listened with both my mind and my ears as I crouched in the stream for a drink. The water swirled around me, and for a moment, I thought I scented blood.

Time to go; the old Alpha had perhaps saved me.

A snap of a branch in the direction I'd left drew my attention.

Then again, perhaps he'd not.

I turned and broke into a run, flying through the bush, leaping rocks, not really caring how much noise I made. They knew I was here.

I glanced back once to see four large males bearing down on me. Four. I couldn't take that many. I veered to the side and started up the side of the ravine, scrambling and pulling at roots in an attempt to move faster.

Kill him.

The words and image were clear. There would be no becoming a part of this pack. With that knowledge I lurched over the top of the ravine's edge. A fence blocked my path. I grabbed the top of it and heaved for all I was worth, pulling myself over.

I fell onto the ground on the other side and stared at my hands, shocked that I could feel them. That I could move them.

A snarl behind me snapped me out of my wonderment. I pushed to my feet and ran toward the house that loomed in front of me. I didn't slow as I approached the door, but tipped my shoulder downward and hit it hard, ramming it open. I fell through the doorway, spun, and looked back.

The males had boosted themselves over the fence and were headed straight for me. I kicked the door shut, not that it caught now that I'd broken it. I ran through the house and found a second door. I broke through that one, then paused.

To my side was a set of stairs going to the second floor of the house. I bolted up them before I could change my mind.

At the top, I flattened myself to the floor and watched the open door. The four Nevermores never slowed as they blasted through the open door and outside, searching for me. I rose to a crouch and slipped down the stairs, through the house and out the back door. To either side of me were more houses and more fences.

Mara was in one direction, and freedom from the world I'd left behind was in the other. I turned my back and headed toward the barracks once more.

Three days of dodging the new pack, three days of little sleep, less food, and constant vigilance. I kept having to backtrack and wait them out which meant getting to the barracks was nowhere near as fast as it should have been.

I'd had to kill two of the pack members who caught me unawares. At least their deaths were quick, that was all I could give them.

When the barracks finally came into view, though, there was much movement. I saw Mara in a Jeep with the kid. They were leaving.

Well then, it was time to follow.

CHAPTER THIRTY - TWO

Mara

The plan Clark came up with seemed like a good one. Clark had two of his men sneak down to the bluffs that rose above Donavan's compound and plant explosives all along the edge. They wouldn't hurt anyone, but they would draw lots of attention to the compound's front entrance.

"You need as many men as you can get to storm the back half of the compound. Missy and I will go with Green as his backup." I had been arguing with both of them for almost three days. I was not going to be left behind. "Besides, I'm no safer here by myself."

"Fine." Clark was reluctant. "But you do what Green says and if he says run, you run."

I gave him a salute. "Yes, sir."

"I mean it, Mara."

"Listen, I'm not staying behind."

The thing was we both knew I was eager to get out and see if Sebastian was close by. I still couldn't believe he hadn't come back. That he'd left.

The morning we were to take the compound dawned with a coolness, dew resting on everything, that reminded me fall was on its way. I made my way slowly up to the rifle range with Missy, as I had whenever I could find a moment, hoping for a sign that Sebastian had maybe come back.

I called for Sebastian, whistled for Scout, but there was no reply. Missy sniffed the ground and searched the area with her tail up but without a single growl or raising of her hackles. That alone told me that there were no Nevermores around.

Even the other packs in the area seemed to have faded into the background. Maybe one of them had taken over Sebastian's pack. What if he was hurt or, worse, dead? I could all too easily imagine Sebastian being chased through the woods, but why in the world would I think he'd carry that old male with no feet?

I shook my head and turned away from the range.

Shudders rippled through me at the thought of Sebastian gone forever—dead or lost to the drug, did it matter which one took him from me? I circled my baby bump with one hand. The thought of being alone, pregnant, and then a single mom in this world was enough to give me full on panic attacks. I took a slow even breath and let it out, counted between breaths and did it again. Losing it right now would not help me at all.

No, it would be all right. Sebastian had to be alive. I believed it; he was out there. I just had to find him.

"Come on, Missy. We've got work to do." I snapped my fingers and she loped back to me with a big floppy grin on her face.

At the bunker, Green waited for me in a Jeep.

"Ready?" He opened the door for Missy and she leapt into the back.

I slid into the passenger's seat. "Yes. Has there been any sign of pack activity?"

"Nothing. Which is super weird, but we're taking it as a sign."

What he meant was Clark was taking it as a sign. More than once Clark had pointed out that with Vincent gone, the Nevermores had never been quieter. I pointed out that he'd also let the biggest draw—the caged Nevermores—go.

The drive to the bluffs was eerily quiet. I'd thought that outside the barracks there would be at least a sign of the Nevermore packs in the area. Missy had her head out the window, enjoying the ride. Again, I looked to her for warning that there were Nevermores close by.

"This is an awfully big city to have so few Nevermores left in it." I stared out the window, for the first time almost wanting to see a flash of yellow.

Green took a left hand turn carefully, weaving around a car left in the road. "Seemed that a lot of people thought they needed to get off the island when everything started to go wrong. I think a lot of them headed to the mainland, maybe in hopes of escape. I don't really know, but we could see them all from up on the base leaving in droves. Taking the ferries like crazy until they shut down."

I frowned. "But if this was ground zero, why wouldn't people stay? Why wouldn't they try to fix things?"

Green shrugged. "You didn't know it was ground zero. Most people didn't realize how close they were to the start of things. It was kept pretty quiet. We only found out from Vincent."

"And you trusted him?"

Green shrugged again. "He worked with the Doc. Donavan. He was on the security detail."

A few short minutes later, we rumbled to a stop. We were just on the outskirts of downtown, on the hill that was at the top of Third Street next to St. Peter's Catholic Church—that being if all the signage was correct.

Green pulled out a map and pointed at it. "Donavan's compound is situated on the harbor, in what was the Port Theatre. Cliff above it has a walk-on access from the back side that is completely cut off from view of the compound."

"A theatre was turned into a compound?"

"You'll understand when you see it. A great hulking concrete thing. Pretty ugly if you ask me."

Green started the Jeep forward again and we headed down the big hill. "As soon as we set off the explosives, we'll get out of there and head back to the bunker. Honestly, I still can't believe Clark let you come along."

I shrugged. "You need a backup. What if something goes wrong, or you get hurt? Clark and the others can't help, and they are depending on you to get the job done. You showed me how to set the explosives off in case something happened, so that's that."

I glanced in the rearview mirror, and saw a flicker of movement. Missy tipped her head back and a low growl slipped past her lips.

A body dashed between buildings, a distinct sheen of yellow on the skin. A shiver crawled up my spine as more bodies ducked and dived. They were stalking us in the Jeep. Shit. Double shit.

"Green, I think we've got company," I said as I continued to watch a very large pack make its way down Third Street using the buildings for cover. I tried to count them, but their scattered groupings made it difficult. "I think it's about twice the size of the pack from the barracks," I said. Which would make sixty or more Nevermores. That was more than the number of men Clark had on hand by more than double.

Green hit the gas and took a sharp right, a left, and then another right. I held on to the handle above my head, grateful for it as I gritted my teeth against the swaying movement of the Jeep. Missy grunted as she slammed around in the backseat.

"Sorry, girl," he said.

"Where are we going? I thought you said the compound was on the harbor?"

"It is, but we need some space between us and this pack, so I'm coming in at a different angle. It should throw them off."

It took us another fifteen minutes to circle around to the south and drive up a small hill and onto a bluff that overlooked the Port Theatre, or more accurately, Donavan's compound. I had to trust that Green had it right because I couldn't see the theatre.

He parked the Jeep and the three of us got out and crept up the slope.

Green pushed his mic tightly against his head, a look of concentration coming over his face, some noise that could have been a voice barely audible to me.

"Got it." He nodded. "Okay, we'll get set here."

I touched his arm and drew his attention to me. "What's happening?"

"They're all in place. Clark will wait on the first explosion before they move in." A bead of sweat dripped down the side of his face. I bit my lower lip and swallowed hard.

His mic buzzed and he pushed it into his ear, and his face quickly shaded red. Slipping it off, he handed it to me. I slipped the headset on and adjusted it.

What was going on? "Hello?"

Clark's voice came through loud and clear. "Be careful, Mara. If at any point you think you and Green have been seen, get the hell out of there. Understand?"

I nodded, forgetting he couldn't see me for a moment. "Got it. Be safe, Clark."

"You too, beautiful."

The headset clicked and I took it off, tangling it in my hair. I cursed at it, using words I reserved for the very worst days of my life. My emotions rioted left and right, and I didn't know what to make of them. I'd never loved anyone like Sebastian, never been with anyone but him. But Clark . . . he was handsome and strong, and he hadn't taken the drug. He was right, it would be easy to fall for him, and that was what scared me. Just how quickly it could happen. But I wasn't going there. Sebastian was waiting for me and I wasn't giving up on him.

While Green got the equipment ready, I crawled forward with Missy and stared at the theatre turned compound. Green was right; it was rather ugly. The base of it was solid windows, good for a theatre, I suppose, but not so good when it came to protecting what was inside. I could see many of them had been shattered, leaving dark holes into the interior. I suppressed a shiver. The gaping wounds in what had once been a place of music and laughter were disturbing. I blinked and shook the feeling off. The theatre was cylindrical in shape and it was at least four, maybe five stories high, surrounded by a large fence like the kind around a construction site. Other than that, I couldn't see what was protecting it.

"You ready?" Green was at my side. I nodded and slipped some earplugs in, and clapped my hands over Missy's ears. Green nodded, opened a cover on a small black box, and flicked a switch.

I held my breath, counted the seconds away.

Nothing.

Green frowned and flicked the switch back and forth several times. Still nothing.

Oh, this was not good.

Green started to talk at a rapid pace into his mouthpiece. I pulled out my earplugs.

". . . check the wiring. They must have set it wrong, the idiots!"

"Isn't that just a tad bit dangerous? Haven't you already flicked the switch to set them off?" I grabbed at Green's arm. "Maybe we should go back and regroup."

It was ridiculous to even think about climbing down the cliff when there were live explosives. We'd just have to retreat and try something else another time.

"Clark is depending on me, Mara. There are only a few boats left in the harbor and we need access to them, as well as to whatever cure Donavan has cooked up." Green's young face looked as though he'd aged in mere moments.

Before I could say anything, he brushed past me and made his way down the ivy-covered cliff, using the greenery for handholds. I peered down after him, watching him. Missy whined softly and I wrapped an arm over her back. "I know, girl. I know."

I put my knuckles to my mouth as Green crept along the outer fence, checking first one small package taped to the metal, and then a second. As he stood at the second package, the first one went off.

Green dropped to the ground and the air shattered around him. I bit down on my knuckles, and swallowed a yell. Metal twisted and screamed in protest. The explosives did their job effectively, tearing a hole in the fence and making enough noise to wake the dead.

Another explosion rocked the air and Missy whimpered and tried to pull back. I couldn't see through the dust, and my ears were ringing from the noise. Where was Green?

Boom after boom rattled and then shouts and gunfire erupted from behind the theatre. All the explosives had gone off, and as the dust cleared, I could see him lying there.

Green was on the ground, unmoving.

I couldn't just leave him.

"Missy, stay." I pointed to the cliff top. She pawed at me as I followed the same goat path Green used. Missy ignored me. "Missy, no!" She slid down the cliff, slammed into my legs, and we both tumbled the last ten feet to the ground. I landed hard on my back, which knocked the wind out of me. All I could think about, though, was the baby. That kind of fall . . . what kind of damage could it do?

I groaned, gulped a big breath and rolled to my side. Missy was there, holding a paw up. I couldn't even be mad at her for knocking us down. She didn't want to be left behind and I could understand that. We limped to Green's side. I placed a hand on his back and let out a sigh of relief when his back rose under my hand.

I rolled him carefully so he was on his back. His eyes were closed, and a trickle of blood dribbled from his nose. "Come on, Green. Get up." How I was going to help him, I had no clue. But I couldn't leave him here.

Missy barked at the same time a voice broke through the buzzing in my ears.

"You there, what are you doing?"

I spun on my haunches to face the partially blasted gates. Behind the twisted metal were several large guns pointed at me by even larger men. They were dressed in black and were wearing sunglasses like a whole crew of bodyguards.

Carefully, I held up my hands. "Please, he's hurt. I need to get him help." Maybe I could appeal to their compassion for other humans. I couldn't see their faces behind the scopes of the guns, but they didn't seem that interested in helping.

"Lower your guns." A man stepped out around the others. He looked to be in his mid-forties, around the same age as Vincent. Slim and wearing nicely creased pants and a polo shirt, he was not dressed as the men holding the guns. He had on wire-rimmed glasses and his hair was neatly combed to one side. This had to be Donavan, the scientist who'd developed Nevermore.

Donavan smiled at me, then made a waving motion with his hands and his men pulled the gates back together, locking us out. "I do believe that we will not need to shoot you after all. Your death is here without our help. Good day."

Missy went wild as she spun, barking and snapping her teeth.

Hands grabbed my arms, the fingers veined in yellow, and I screamed as the Nevermore behind me roared. I twisted hard to the left and snapped myself out of his hands.

A second Nevermore launched himself at me. I was in a half crouch and I stood, using the momentum to swing my foot in a hard kick. I connected a solid blow to his left knee which dropped him to the ground with a howl. I did a slow spin. One side of us was the bluff. The other side was the compound which curled around, blocking the third possible direction. That only left the waterfront. But from the edges of the harbor crept a large pack—I assumed the one that had been dogging us on our way here. At my feet, Green began to stir.

"Green! If you can hear me, wake up!" I screamed at him, knowing it didn't really matter how much noise we made now. The pack had seen us.

Green didn't answer with his voice, but with his gun. The Nevermores nearest me dropped as he emptied his clip. There was still nowhere for us to run. The pack pushed Missy and me against the tall fence, and Donavan and his men were on the other side, guns in hand, waiting for me to be eaten. Green scrambled to his feet, knocked down a Nevermore who grabbed for him, and ran in the opposite direction, back toward the cliff. His gait was unsteady but he kept upright.

I pressed my back into the hard wire, my heart galloping as gunfire continued to go off in the distance. I hoped that Clark made it in to the compound, but even if he did, there was no way he would make it to me in time. Missy stayed in front of me, lunging and snapping even with her hurt leg.

The pack circled around, leaping in to push, poke

and pinch me. I didn't understand at first why they weren't attacking me.

I dropped to the ground. "Missy, here!" I called her to me and wrapped my arms around her. I tucked my legs under me as the pack continued to close ranks on us.

One young female came close enough that I was able to land a solid punch, catching her in an upper-cut to the jaw that knocked her backward. The pack stilled and removed their hands from me.

"What are you doing, eh? Or more importantly, *what* are you?" Donavan called to me.

I didn't answer him, didn't have time to think about much of anything. What I assumed was the Alpha of this pack pushed his way through to me. He was at least as big as Sebastian, maybe even a bit taller, and easily as well muscled. With a single swift move, he hauled me to my feet and stuck his nose against my neck, breathing deeply. I kept a hand down, press-ing Missy away from him. I tried to think back to the last time I'd showered and knew it had been before Seraphima came into the world, however brief her stay might have been. I stunk like Sebastian and the other Nevermore pack.

I held perfectly still, but as the Alpha got more ag-gressive with his sniffing, it quickly turned into lick-ing. He gave me no choice. I hit him the chest with the flat of my hand. "No!" He dropped me with a startled look, his eyes wide with what could only be shock that I'd spoken to him.

The moment paused, stretching like taffy before once more erupting into action.

Gunfire roared around us and two Jeeps sped into view with men I didn't recognize driving. My heart sunk; Clark hadn't breached the compound and his Jeeps had been hijacked—that was the only answer to what I was seeing.

The Nevermores began to fall as Donavan's men shot them. I hit the ground, grabbed Missy and covered us as best I could. A heavy body landed on top of me, squishing us down.

Soft, warm breath tickled on the back of my neck and my whole body shook. A large, very familiar pair of hands wrapped themselves around me and circled my belly as he pulled me tightly against a body I knew as well as I knew my own.

"Sebastian," I breathed.

"Love too," he breathed the words into my ear and held me close. I had no idea where he'd come from, or why he'd stayed away so long—and at that moment, I didn't care. The Jeeps went roaring by, then they sped through an opening in the gate that was quickly closed by the men standing guard.

Sebastian jumped up and pulled me to my feet. He wasn't fast enough. The Alpha male roared a challenge that Bastian couldn't deny and he spun, placing me behind him, as they launched at one another.

Hands grabbed me and I spun to see the red-headed young male, Buck, pulling at me. I followed him, dodging the bodies and using the smoke for cover as the sound of gunfire once more reached my ears. Bullets cut through the air around us and I ducked each time, hoping I was doing the right thing. Hoping I wouldn't get hit.

Buck dragged me along until something bit into me and I stumbled, my left leg suddenly numb. A brilliant haze of pain forced me to my knees. "Stop, I have to stop."

I reached down and touched the back of my left calf. A dart stuck out of my leg. I pulled it, but it was too late to stop whatever they'd put into the dart from going into my veins. The world around me fuzzed over, the noises dimmed, and the light softened. I felt nothing but the agony of fire in my leg and realization that I'd gone from the frying pan into the fire.

Hands slapped over my mouth and a pinch in my arm competed for my attention. Wire-rimmed glasses and perfectly smoothed hair came into view as Donavan leaned over me.

"Well, well, well. Beauty loves her Beast, but will 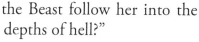 the Beast follow her into the depths of hell?"

CHAPTER
THIRTY - THREE

Sebastian

The fight didn't last long. The other male was big, but stupid. I sent him an image of another Nevermore sneaking up behind him and he spun. I grabbed him around the neck and strangled him. I held him tightly until he stopped struggling, but by then . . .

I ran for the compound as the men carried Mara inside. I pounded at the fence, searching for a way in. But already the openings that had been there were gone, patched up with extra fencing. I dug my fingers into the thin wire and contemplated climbing over.

No . . . that wouldn't do. There were too many men, too many guns. I paced around the compound, searching, though, unable to leave.

The sight of Mara being courted by the other Alpha had been too much. The image had unleashed the tight hold I kept on the part of me that was all Nevermore. I struggled with the rage and the desire to kill things, to eat anything in front of me.

The only thing I could keep my mind on was getting to Mara. Mara would help me find myself again.

CHAPTER THIRTY - FOUR

Mara

I floated in a strange fog between awake and asleep for some time. I'd start to wake up, and then would fall back into the dreams that chased me around and around. Where was I, and what was I doing here? The sounds and smells that assaulted me were not ones I recognized. I wasn't in the barracks.

Was I at home on the farm? No, that wasn't right either. My eyelids flickered open and I found my-self staring up at a chandelier that was swaying ever so slightly. My one hand hung off where I lay and a tongue licked it. "Missy." I said her name softly and she gave a thump of her tail as she butted her head into my hand. At least, I had her still.

"I'm telling you, she's infected and we should keep her with the rest of the Nevermores downstairs. It's only a matter of time before she changes, you know that. How the hell she got a shot so late in the game doesn't matter. It's obvious, she's one of them." I didn't recognize the voice.

"No, no. You don't understand, Clint. The pack was trying to protect her, like she's one of them, but she's obviously human. There are no turning signs in her at all. This could be the breakthrough in our research. I think she's taken the drug, but her system has overcome it. This is what could save Juliana," Donavan said, his voice soft yet very excited.

A shuffle of feet. "I still don't think it's a good idea. Either one of those big bastards might break in to get to her."

That made me groan, and though I didn't feel strong enough to sit up, I croaked out, "Sebastian, is he okay?"

A face came into view—Donavan's—and I got an up-close look at his bright blue eyes behind his glasses. He smiled down at me, but the smile didn't reach anything but the edge of his lips. Clark had said Donavan was unstable, but not cruel. Staring into his face, I could believe it. Donavan's eyelids twitched as he looked down on me, his eyes flicking first one way and then the other, seemingly unable to be still.

"I don't know a Sebastian." He paused and fussed the edge of the sheet that covered me. "I am, however, glad to see you're awake. Do you have a name, dear?" He offered me his hand to help me sit up. I didn't take it and instead forced myself into a sitting position on my own with a hiss of pain as my leg protested the movement.

"My name's Mara. Do I have a bullet in me?" I touched the bandage wrapped around my upper calf.

Donavan smiled at me. "No, Mara, what hit you is a type of tranquilizer dart we use to drop the Nevermores at a safe distance so they can be brought in without damage to them."

"Will the drugs hurt my baby?" I asked, my hand going to my belly, my eyes searching his face, not trusting him to tell me the truth.

He tipped his head from side to side and his fingers flicked at unseen things. "They shouldn't. We will run some blood work and perhaps do an ultrasound if you'd like to check." The skin of his face twitched and his smile tightened. I swallowed hard. I was not safe here any more than I'd been safe with Vincent in the barracks.

From what I overheard, I had no doubt that part of the blood work he wanted done was to see if I'd taken Nevermore, to see if my system had the antibodies or whatever it was he was looking for, but I didn't care. "That would be good. I'm about fifteen weeks along now, I think," I said, as I started to get up. "I need to see where my husband is. He was in the pack out there."

Donavan shook his head. "No. There is no contact outside the gate. It's not safe. Lie down and we'll bring the ultrasound in." I struggled against his hands, though I was tired and my efforts were ineffectual.

He sighed. "Perhaps you could describe your husband to me. Maybe he's in the morgue already." Donavan patted the bed beside me as if that was some comfort, but otherwise didn't touch me. Chills swept through me, but I refused to buckle under the possibility that Sebastian dead.

"Sebastian is 6'4", has dark hair and very wide shoulders. He has scars on his right leg where . . ." I almost said where Vincent burned him, but held back, "he was burned. He was the new male fighting the Alpha of the pack before I got shot." I watched his eyes and recognition filtered through the madness in them.

"Ah, yes, he's still alive and quite, oh shall we say, pissed? The last time I saw him he was circling the compound and pounding on the gate."

"Please, don't hurt him," I whispered, remembering the explosion all too vividly, the spray of bodies on the ground. "He'll listen to me; I can bring him in. Please, let me go get him."

Donavan's jaw twitched. "We brought most of the pack in; we don't shoot them like Vincent's crew does." Apparently, he didn't know Vincent hadn't been shooting them lately, but instead, torturing them.

I frowned. "Then what was that explosion, all the smoke, and the bodies everywhere?"

"A canister of tear gas, a light bomb and then a spray of fast-acting sedative darts. The other explosions were from Vincent's crew." His fingers flexed and danced on the edge of the bed.

"What do you want with the pack?" I asked, though I already thought I knew the answer.

Donavan bobbed his head while he smiled and steepled his fingers. "We'll run blood work on all of them to see if there are any anomalies. It's the only way we will be able to find a better cure. The sedatives are not working on the two big males, not at all." He grimaced, then his eyes brightened and a very bad feeling washed through me. "They may only help us once they are dead."

"Wait," I held a hand out to him. "If . . . you think his blood could change things, couldn't it? You wouldn't have to kill him, would you?"

He lifted an eyebrow at me. "Perhaps I could consider letting him live if he were of enough help to me."

I thought quickly. I couldn't trust Donavan, that much was certain, but my mind kept circling back to the cure. If there was one, as the rumors persisted, it would be here. There had to be something better than what Vincent had used on Adam and Eve, the two shuffling Nevermores who looked as though they'd been lobotomized.

At that moment, it was the best I could do, and I would take the offer for what it was worth. I reminded myself that at least Sebastian was alive. I nodded, my eyes glued to a dark stain on the floor. "I can bring him in. He'll give blood. Just don't hurt him."

"Excellent. You first, though, dear." Donavan attempted to pat my arm, missed and touched my hip. He jumped as though he'd been scalded. He hurried out with the man I assumed was Clint at his side.

They were replaced by a woman, the first I'd seen in a long time that wasn't a Nevermore. Her name tag on her starched white nurse's uniform said "Lucy." She wrapped my arm with a plastic band and flicked at a vein in the crook of my elbow until it came to the surface. I stared at the ceiling and the sparkly chandelier, wincing as she jabbed me none too gently with the needle.

"You didn't take Nevermore?" I asked, just wanting to speak with another woman who wasn't trying to eat me. Even if she was on Donavan's side.

She frowned down at me, her face a sharp twist of unhappiness. "I hadn't put together enough money for it when the true nature of it reared its ugly head. Pure dumb luck. You?"

"I'm allergic to Scotch broom. The doctor said it would kill me if I took it. Kind of squashed my plans of getting pregnant."

Lucy stared at me, and then pulled up a chair as she drew the blood. "But you're pregnant now? That seems beyond stupid to get knocked up at a time like this."

I gave a half laugh, not taking offense at all. "My husband took the drug when the fertility tests came back that he was the problem, not me. I didn't know he took it. We were trying but not really."

"Luck went one way for me, other way for you." She reached around me and grabbed another empty vial that she plunked onto the end of the needle. After three more full vials, she pulled the needle out of my arm and pressed a cotton ball onto the open vein.

"Hold, here for at least two minutes. I'll be back to put a bandage on in a bit." She stood to leave, her frazzled brunette hair tied into a messy bun.

I pressed my fingers against the cotton ball. "Can I ask you a question?"

"You can ask, and I'll answer if I can." She turned at the doorway, impatience highlighted in her hand on her hip, and the arch of her eyebrow. I wondered if perhaps we were the only human women left on Vancouver Island. That was a horrible thought.

"Is Donavan as bad as Vincent made him out to be?"

"I don't know how Vincent made him out to be. But genius often comes in the guise of madness. Right now, we need a genius to make this mess right again, to get all our people back."

"Is there a cure?" I asked. Clark had thought so. I prayed he was right.

She shook her head. "He's close to a breakthrough, but that's all I know. I just help him."

Lucy left the room, but locked the door behind her. My eyes closed slowly, in what I thought was a blink, but when they opened, she was back in the room puttering. I must have fallen asleep.

"Mara, they're bringing the ultrasound in now. Drink this, it'll help us see the baby clearly." She held out a glass to me and I took it, grateful for the cool clean liquid. "Was I asleep?"

Lucy grimaced. "You slept right through the night, didn't move a muscle, not even when I put a bandage on your arm. I should know, they made me sit in here and keep a watch on you."

I swallowed hard, shocked. All night? A lot of things could happen in one night. "Is Sebastian still acting up?"

"The big boy? Donavan's tried to talk to him, see if he can get a response out of him like you said you could."

"How's it going?" I asked as I sat up slowly, the room spinning slightly.

She shook her head, her earrings catching the light and throwing rainbow prisms around the room. "Not as well as he'd hoped, not as bad as he thought."

"That's enough now, Lucy, we don't want to work up our young mother here." Donavan stepped into the room and Lucy swallowed hard.

Missy was quiet under the bed, though I knew she was still there. She kept butting my hand with her head to get me to scratch her.

Donavan sat in front of me. The skin around his eyes twitched and the muscles in his face followed suit. He seemed to get a hold of himself finally. "Your Sebastian wouldn't talk to me, but last night when I said your name, he calmed down and stopped the rioting. Fascinating, really, very unusual for the species to behave in such a manner. I've never seen any of them respond to past memory stimulus. I don't know if your Sebastian made it through the night." He lifted an eyebrow, watching my reaction as one would inspect a strange insect, a morbid mixture of curiosity and revulsion.

I held his gaze and my breath. Slowly I let the air out. I would not believe that Sebastian was gone until I saw the body myself. Until then, I chose to believe he was alive and well. Lucy came to stand over me, a tube of something in her hand. "I'm going to put some gel on you and then we can take a look at the baby."

Donavan shook his head. "No. You said you would bring your husband in, and you want to see your baby to make sure it's a viable fetus. Get your husband first. I want to run tests on him, and the sedative darts haven't worked on him as well as I would like. If he's dead, then call in the other big male; he seemed taken with you as well."

My stomach rolled at the thought of Sebastian being dead, the possibility higher than ever before with the matched size and strength of the other male. I licked my lips and nodded slowly. "Okay."

Donavan continued to smile and nodded as if he expected nothing else. Lucy let out an audible sigh of relief and I stared at her. What was her game in this anyway?

The two of them guided me to the front door and then all but shoved me forward.

"If you can't bring him in, I will have him shot. If you try to run, I will have him shot. If you think to call your friends . . ."

"I get it," I said. "You'll shoot him. No need to spell it out, Einstein."

Donavan laughed as if I'd hit the punch line in a joke. "No, no. I won't shoot him for that. Your friends are all dead, so there will be no need to try and call them. You are quite the tart, aren't you?" He laughed again as he shut the door and locked it behind me.

I started out across the tiled courtyard to the front gate, limping ever so slightly. The spot where the dart had stuck me throbbed in time with my blood pumping.

"Sebastian." My voice echoed down and over the water. The few ships moored there bobbed along with the gentle roll of the waves. It was peaceful considering how short a time ago it had been a war zone in this very spot.

I made it all the way to the fence without any movement. I called out again and waited. Nothing. My heart began to pound. What if he'd left me here, believing me safe, believing me better off without him? I didn't think I could go through that again.

"Sebastian!" I screamed, my fear giving me more decibels than normal.

I limped along the fence line toward the bluffs Green and I had stood on. I kept calling for Sebastian and still there was no response. As a last resort I let out a whistle, hoping for Scout.

There was a shift in the bushes at the base of the cliffs and my hopes rose. Scout pulled himself out of the shrubs and literally crawled to the fence. I crouched down and put my hands through, touching his face. It was obvious he was hurt badly; his left leg was at an odd angle and his body was a mass of bruises. Through his right bicep was a gunshot wound that had crusted over.

"I'm so sorry," I whispered, emotions clogging my throat. I stood and half ran to the nearest gate. I slipped through and locked it behind me. Missy bounced on that side of the fence while I ran to Scout's side. He grimaced when I helped him to sit up and propped him against the fence. "Sebastian, where is he?"

Scout shook his head and my throat tightened.

An image of the fight between the two males flashed through my mind. Of one being killed, but I couldn't tell which. There was too much smoke. I put a hand to my head. I was going crazy, there was no way I could know what happened.

Bastian wasn't dead. I refused to believe that was what Scout was trying to tell me. He pushed himself to stand and hobbled on his broken leg toward the water. I followed, trying to decipher what it was he was trying to show me. A shot rang out and a bullet ricochet off the pavement in front of me. Scout dove for cover behind the nearest bush and I held up my hands.

"I wasn't trying to leave!"

Apparently, I wasn't to go toward the harbor.

There was another shuffle of bush and Scout scuttled away down the water line, dragging his broken leg behind him. I scrubbed my face with my hands, emotions welling up hard and fast. So much for my help there. I hoped Scout would be okay.

As my strength began to wane, I turned and called for Sebastian again. I walked slowly as I favored my leg.

A scan of the area nearly stopped my breath. There was a hand and arm sticking out from under one of the green hedges. I forced myself to run to where the body lay. The hair was the wrong color. It was the Alpha male that Sebastian had been fighting. His guts were ripped out of him, spread in a semi-circle where the ravens and crows had made their feast.

Was this what happened to Sebastian? Had he died alone and in pain, keening for me? A sob ripped from my throat as I turned and familiar hands grabbed my arms.

Sebastian let out a low rumble, a wild look in his eye that I ignored as I threw myself at him, great gulping sobs of relief pouring out of me. "You're here, I knew you weren't dead. I knew it."

At first, he didn't respond, and then slowly he slid his arms around me and buried his nose in the crook of my neck. Warm wet tears slid down the skin of my neck and dripped into my shirt, leaving a warm streak wherever the tears fell.

I clung to him, the razor edge of fear sharp on my heart leaving me more than a little needy. I was terrified to lose him again. "Sebastian, come with me, please." I took his hand and walked to the gate. He stared at the high fence and stopped dead in his tracks. I didn't blame him, the memory of Vincent and the captivity in that camp was too fresh. But we didn't have a choice. I knew that Donavan would shoot us both if we tried to run.

I didn't know how else to explain it so I took his

hand and placed it on my belly. "Please. This is for us, for all of us. The man here can help if we let him."

He closed his eyes and a tremble rippled through him. I pulled on his hand and he stepped forward with me, slowly, but moving. A scuffle to our right snapped us both into high alert. It was Buck watching us go inside the fence with a look of disbelief. Sebastian grunted at him and flung his hand as if tossing Buck something. Buck nodded and slipped back down the slope towards the water.

"You just made him Alpha, didn't you?"

Sebastian nodded once and then touched my cheek with his hand. He had given up his leadership over a second pack to be with me, his love overriding the animal drive to be Alpha.

My eyes filled and we walked into Donavan's compound together, holding hands, ready to face whatever would come our way.

Chapter Thirty - Five

Sebastian

The other Nevermores had whispered to me the truth of the place I walked into. This was where death waited. More so than Vincent, this was where Nevermores went in and disappeared forever. But Mara needed me. Our child needed me.

And this was where she said we had to go.

So I would follow her.

Always.

CHAPTER THIRTY - SIX

Mara

"I hope you're sure of this, Donavan, bringing a Nevermore in here un-se-dated," Lucy whispered to herself as Sebastian and I walked past her. He glared at her but otherwise didn't make a single move in her direction. I clung to his hand as fear bubbled through me. I had no illusions about what would happen to Sebastian if he went after one of the other people in this compound.

The men all carried guns and they, like Clark's men, knew how to use them.

I followed Lucy to the room I'd started in and now held the ultrasound machine. Donavan was still there. He didn't look up when we came in.

"No doubt your Sebastian wasn't as malleable as you'd hoped. Mara, it isn't your fault, my wife Juliana is the love of my life and she attacks the cage whenever I come near . . ." His words stuttered to a stop as he lifted his eyes and saw us standing hand in hand in the doorway.

"This is Sebastian." I smiled up at my scowling husband. I squeezed his hand. "Sebastian, this is Donavan. He might have a cure for Nevermore."

Sebastian's eyes narrowed, then he looked down at me and the wildness ebbed. He lowered his head and pressed it against mine.

Donavan cleared his throat, his smile gone, his eyes narrowed almost as much as Sebastian's had been. "Ultrasound first, then, as I am a man of my word. After that I will draw blood from the male." His voice was colder than it had been, even for him, and there was a sharp edge to it now. What was wrong? Why was he angry? I would have thought that having Sebastian here would have made him ecstatic.

I didn't let go of Bastian, and he helped me on to the table. I clung to his hand, holding him as close as I could. A few moments later Lucy came back in, slightly pale, but still doing as Donavan wanted.

She said nothing and the silence was heavy and full of fear, the air around us seeming to thicken, clogging my throat. I pulled up my shirt and pushed my pants down a bit to reveal the bump that was growing faster and faster.

The gel was cold and I sucked in a lungful of air. At Sebastian's concerned look I smiled. "Just cold."

He nodded, and then Lucy swirled the ultrasound on my bump and a picture came up on the screen.

"There's the head, I think," she said and shifted the position. "And there's the heart beating away."

A staccato not unlike the thrum of humming-bird wings rushed over the ultrasound and I held my breath. Sebastian stared at the screen, then looked at my belly and back again. Emotions filled me and started to spill over into tears I'd been holding back. "That's our baby," I said.

"Always," Sebastian breathed the word.

"Always love," I whispered back.

Donavan stood, a look on his face as though he were being strangled, and left the room. He slammed the door behind him. Sebastian turned and stared at the door, a calculating look in his eyes. Missy crept out from under the bed and pressed herself against Bastian's leg. He dropped a hand to her head and scrubbed her behind the ears.

I tried not to make too much of it, but . . . it seemed like a huge step. Both for Missy to see he was coming around and for him to not try and eat her.

Lucy blanched as she stared at me. "He really does love you, doesn't he?"

I smiled back. "Yes, more than I ever imagined." I paused, took a breath, and asked a question that had been burning in the back of my mind. "Donavan is trying to bring his wife back, isn't he?"

Lucy stopped what she was doing and looked at me, finally giving me a slow nod. "Juliana is the whole reason he's doing this. They were married for nearly twenty years, childhood sweethearts. But she doesn't remember him at all. Just like the rest of them don't remember their family. It's why I'm here. To help him find the cure." There was more than sorrow in her voice; bitterness lay heavy on her words as she all but glared at me and Sebastian.

"Seeing me and Sebastian together hurts you, doesn't it?"

Again she nodded. I closed my eyes and imagined what it would have been like if Bastian had forgotten me and stayed with Jessica. The pain at the mere thought was instantaneous and overwhelming. I understood why people resented us.

Lucy went back to the ultrasound and slid it across my belly. She stopped over a section I thought might be the baby's tummy, but was hard for me to tell with the slight movement that continued through the whole session.

"Hmm." Lucy's eyes narrowed, and she slid the reader to the left.

"What? Is something wrong?" My heart instantly sped up at the concern on Lucy's face. Sebastian picked up on my anxiety and leaned forward, his face tight with worry.

"I don't know, Mara. The baby is healthy, but I'm just not sure. I have to get Donavan back in here. I don't use this enough to be able to tell exactly what I'm seeing. I'm sure it's nothing." She put the ultrasound down and left the room.

I started to shake. Not again, I couldn't go through losing another baby, not so soon after losing Seraphima. Please God, don't let this happen to us again. I tried to console myself with the fact that we'd heard the heartbeat. This baby was alive; he was a fighter.

I covered my face with my hands and Sebastian leaned over me so he could cradle my head to his chest, hiding me while I sobbed. I tried to pull myself together, I did, but it was hard. It felt as though every time the world started to give us a chance, the rug was yanked out from under us again.

Bastian and Missy let out a tandem growl. Donavan cleared his throat and I pushed Bastian gently away from me. The tears stopped in an instant.

"I'm sure it's nothing," he said, smiling at me and placing the ultrasound back on my belly. I grimaced as his fingertips brushed across my skin here and there. I was not comforted by him in the least.

He moved the ultrasound first to the left and then to the right and back again, his grin never slipping.

"What's wrong with the baby?" I asked, my anxiety getting the better of me.

Donavan turned the machine off and Lucy wiped my belly with a cloth. "The baby seems to have some deformities. It isn't apparent what exactly the final outcome will be, but I have no doubt they are a result of the Nevermore drug. You did conceive this child after Sebastian took the shot?"

I nodded, my heart numb to what he was saying. I licked my lips, trying to work up the spit to ask the question. "But the baby is okay? I'm not going to lose the baby?"

Donavan shook his head slowly. "I don't think so. But it looks as if it has extra limbs. At least one extra arm for sure. Something I've seen on a few of the Nevermores. It's rare but does happen."

I let out a sigh and leaned back on the table. Sebastian stared from me to Donavan and back again. "It's okay, the baby is going to be okay." I had to trust in that, had to believe I wouldn't lose this child, or my husband. I had to force away the fear of an extra arm on my child.

Donavan left the room and Sebastian and I were alone. He bent, laid his ear on my tummy and I put my hand on his head, running my fingers through his dark hair.

Moments later, Lucy came in, needle and vial in her hand. "I need to draw blood and then I'll take you to your room."

I got Sebastian to sit and Lucy was able to draw blood quickly from him. He didn't even flinch when she jabbed the needle in. I glared at her and she staved off my words with a wave of her hand. "Their skin is thicker than ours, more like hide. There has to be some force or the needle won't go in, so no need to give me the stink eye, girl."

I gritted my teeth and contented myself with stroking Sebastian's other hand, tracing the veins and patterns under his skin. Missy sat between us, alternating leaning against me and then against Sebastian.

"There," Lucy said as she drew the needle out. "We're all done."

I stood and she waved for us to follow her.

I didn't have to ask Missy to follow. She heeled between us, her eyes taking everything in. I took

Sebastian's hand and gripped it tightly as if by sheer force I could keep him here with me. I was deathly afraid to be separated from him yet again. Even if it meant I would be caged like an animal, I didn't care.

Lucy led us upstairs, which surprised me. The theatre still had much of the local and native artwork on the walls, but that didn't hide its utilitarian looks. Everything was cement. Walls, floor, ceiling. Maybe it was for acoustics or maybe just a cost issue, but either way, it was rather stark. We stopped on the third level and took a door down a long hallway. It opened into the hotel that sat next to the theatre. From there Lucy took us to a nice, clean room on the third floor.

"Don't know why you get this room, but here it is. The water works, but don't expect it to be hot." We stepped inside and she shut the door, locking it behind her.

Alone with Sebastian, I stripped out of my clothes and walked to the bathroom. I didn't care if the water was cold; I just wanted to be clean. I think it had been nearly a week since my first and last shower in the bunker.

I cranked the water on, fully intending to have a bath. I could pretend I was camping at the lake or something.

As the tub filled, I peeked into the main room to see Sebastian sitting on the floor, his back against the wall so he could stare at the bedroom door. His breathing was rapid, his chest rising and falling so fast I thought for a moment he might be having a heart attack.

"Bastian?" I ran to his side and dropped to my knees. His arms encircled me and he held on to me as he gulped down great gasps of air. It took me a moment to realize he was crying, sobbing so hard, he could barely get air in to breathe past the emotions.

I closed my eyes and held him.

Images flickered through my mind.

My fault, the child is crippled and it is my fault.

"No, no, there is no blame." I kissed his cheek. "Bastian, there is no blame here." I tried not to think too hard about the fact I'd just seen images in my mind and translated them into words.

"Babe," I took his face in my hands, stared into his yellow eyes, and stroked my fingers across the skin that was as familiar to me as it had been when he was human. "It doesn't matter. The baby will be alive and will be with us. And we will love him no matter how he looks."

Tears streamed from his eyes as his chest continued to heave and he shook his head, hiccupping hard enough to shake his body.

Chapter Thirty – Seven

Sebastian

It would have been better if I'd left her when I knew the shot would turn me. It would have been better if I'd never touched her. If I'd left her while I still could. Anger at myself, at my selfishness, consumed me.

She would be better off without me. Even now, she would not be here if not for the belief that the cure resided in these halls. She would not have been taken to Vincent's barracks if not for the connection between her and me. Maybe he would have left her alone.

The pack would have left her alone if I'd let the drug take me.

But none of that could change this moment now. From here on out, I had to push her away. I was destroying her life with every choice I made.

She deserved better, and the only way to make sure she had that was for me to no longer be here.

I just had to say goodbye one last time.

CHAPTER THIRTY - EIGHT

Mara

"Babe," I whispered. It was the third morning of our stay in the compound. Sebastian grunted and rolled over in his sleep, giving me his back. I traced the yellow lines that made up the shadowy tattoos, the tingle in my fingertips no longer from the Scotch broom in his blood and skin. I followed the lines down to his hips, swirling my finger over each whirl of the plant. Donavan had Lucy take blood from both of us every day, morning and night. I don't know if it was helping his research, but for the moment we were useful to him and that kept us alive and relatively safe.

Sebastian grunted and scooted away from me. I slapped him hard on the hip, snapping him awake. He rolled over and frowned at me. I glared at him.

"I'm allowed to touch you."

His frown deepened and he got out of bed.

"I mean it, Sebastian."

Ignoring me, he walked to the window and stared out, the view over the harbor something he would watch for hours on end while hardly moving a muscle. This was not the Sebastian I knew. Not even the Nevermore Sebastian. Something had changed in him, and I didn't think it was the drug.

I got up and went to stand beside him, to see what it was he was looking at.

What was left of the pack milled about as they scavenged for food amongst the docks, staying far from the water. They screamed if even a single small wave splashed against them. Clark had said they were too dense, that they sunk. That had to be the reason behind the fear of the water. But at the moment, that was the least of my worries.

I swallowed hard. "Do you miss them?"

Sebastian shook his head, then nodded and shrugged his shoulders. I wondered what it was like for him, living between the two worlds, not really human, not really a Nevermore. I had a feeling that if it took much longer for the cure, there was a chance I could still lose him. That the pull of his instincts strengthened every day. The call of the pack and the wildness in him was more than apparent as it battled against the love for me he held onto.

I slipped on my clothes and banged on the bedroom door 'til Lucy came and opened it. Her bedroom was two doors down from ours, so she could keep an eye on us. "What is it?" she asked, her hair dishevelled and her eyes at half-mast.

"I need to speak to Donavan." I pushed my way past her and ran through the long hallway and down the three flights of stairs.

The basement of the theatre was where the lab had been set up. It was easy to find, even though I'd never been there. Despite the early hour, Donavan was already up tinkering away at his tests.

I began to pace the room. "He's slipping further away from me, Donavan. How soon before you have something ready? You've been testing nonstop since we've been here."

Donavan smiled, tucked his hands behind him, and paced a small circle around me. "Do you think you're the only one who's lost a loved one to Nevermore?" he snapped at me, though his grin never slipped and his tone was far from congenial.

I flushed. "Of course not, but—"

"Then what the hell makes you think I would go to the ends of the earth for your precious Sebastian? I'm doing this for *Juliana*, to bring her back to me. If the antibodies *he* carries can help me find a cure, then he is valuable to me, and *only* then," he bit out through his grinning lips.He walked up to me, his face twisted with jealousy and frustration. "The only reason you and Sebastian are being treated as well as you are is simple. You two are my only hope for some sort of breakthrough. If Sebastian is slipping away, then he is of no more use to me than any of the other Nevermores."

"What are you saying?" I asked, a whisper of foreboding passing over me.

"If Sebastian is not the link I need to find the cure, then I'll dispose of him as I have all the other Nevermores. We don't feed the monsters, Mara. We can't afford to."

"You feed Juliana," I said, though in fact, I didn't know that. I'd never seen his wife.

"She's different."

"So is Sebastian," I countered.

We stared at each other, only a foot between us. I wouldn't back down. I owed it to Bastian to fight for him. I owed it to our child to try and save his father.

"We'll draw more blood today and see if the cell count is different. Perhaps he's not changing at all; perhaps he's just giving up on being human. Depression would be a natural response to having the cognitive skills of a human, but being trapped in a monster's body." Donavan turned and slipped on a lab coat and safety glasses, ending our conversation.

I ran back up to our bedroom. Lucy sat in a chair by the door, waiting to see me in. She didn't even look up as I strode past her. I closed the door behind me. Sebastian paced the room, every few steps shaking his head.

God, if I could only know what he was thinking. Wait . . . maybe I could.

I focused on Sebastian, tried to . . . I don't know what I tried to do, but it didn't work. A tired laugh escaped me.

I leaned against the door, as Lucy locked it once

more. Sebastian stopped his pacing and stared at me, his bare chest rising and falling evenly with each breath. I couldn't lift my eyes to him so I stared at the hollow of his throat. If Sebastian didn't hold the key to the cure, Donavan would kill him and I couldn't let that happen.

"Sebastian," I whispered. "We have to go. We have to find a way to escape."

He walked over to me and put a hand on either side of the door, effectively caging me with his body. He let out a low growl and placed his lips on the side of my neck, then nipped at the skin lightly. He brought his hands up to touch my shoulders, then ran them down to my arms to my fingertips. Pressing his body against mine, he put his lips to my ear.

"Love always, Mara."

I couldn't hold the tears back and I wrapped my arms around his neck, clinging to him. I wouldn't lose him, not when we'd both fought so hard to be together.

We tumbled backward onto the bed, my clothes disappearing in a rush of desperation to touch one another. For a moment, the intimacy pushed the fear back, leaving only a blazing fire of love and desire that burned hot enough to scare away the dark that was coming.

I lay in his arms, body tingling, heart racing, and I knew what I had to do.

Lucy was my only hope. I'd seen how she stared at Donavan, her eyes soft and full of emotion. Maybe she could convince him to change his mind, to help me keep Sebastian safe. If she believed in love, she would help me fight for it, wouldn't she?

"I need to speak to Lucy," I whispered into his ear and kissed the edge. He reached up and stroked my face, his other hand pressed against my breast, distracting me. Most effectively. I smiled, and then moaned as he began to work my body over, his gaze never leaving mine. "Sebastian, I have to . . ."

I gave up and surrendered to his touch, the whisper of his lips on mine, the brush of skin tingling with passion.

When I was finally able to untangle myself from Sebastian, the sun was high and I had the beginnings of a plan. My body still humming with Sebastian's caresses, I banged on the door until it opened. "What now?" Lucy grumbled.

"Can I talk to you? Please?"

"We are talking. You look a little flushed," she said, her eyes roving over my reddened skin, rough from teeth and hands.

"Yeah, I'm okay." I cleared my throat. "I need to talk to you about Donavan."

Lucy blinked and her eyes widened. "Why?"

"He's going to kill Sebastian if the key to the cure isn't in the next round of blood work."

Lucy stepped back to let me through. "I'm not surprised. It's what he does."

I fell into step beside her as we walked down the circular hallway. "I know, but I made the mistake of saying that I was worried about Sebastian slipping. It was a moment I can't take back, even though it isn't true."

Lucy shook her head, messy bun bobbing slightly. "What do you want me to do about it?"

I took a deep breath. "I know how you feel about Donavan; I see it in your eyes. Keep him distracted while we try to get away. Help me escape. You know as well as I do there is no cure. Juliana isn't coming back, and killing Sebastian won't change that."

She flushed, her face going bright pink, but then she let out a strangled laugh. "You think I haven't been trying to distract him, honey? There was only one time and he was plastered. It was right after Juliana tried to kill him. Donavan's as devoted to her as you are to Sebastian. You think someone could seduce you away from your man?"

I thought of Clark and slowly shook my head. "No. I suppose you're right."

I stopped and rubbed my face, burying my hands into my hair. What the hell were we going to do?

"I didn't say I wouldn't help you. I just don't think I can seduce him. Here," she handed me a key. "This will get you outside, but from there, you're on your own."

I tucked the key into my jeans pocket. "I don't know when, but we'll leave as quickly as we can. I don't want to test Donavan's patience, or his sanity."

I walked back upstairs to our room only to find it empty, the door wide open. My heart pounding, I searched the room. There was no way Sebastian would have left without me.

Donavan.

I turned and ran back down the stairs, scrambling at each landing to pick up speed. As I reached the bottom floor, I heard raised voices, and then a roar of anger from Sebastian.

"Please, please, please," I whispered under my breath, not entirely sure if I was pleading for more speed or to make it to the lab before Donavan did anything he couldn't take back.

The door to the lab was open and I ran through, but skidded to a halt at the scene before me. Clint and two other men were breathing hard, bent over at the waist, blood splattered here and there.

"He's a fighter. Went fine when we said you were waiting down here for him; soon as he saw you wasn't, he went wild." Clint spoke between deep breaths, but he was not where my eyes rested.

Sebastian was strapped to a metal table, an IV hooked up to his left arm.

Donavan stepped out from behind the other men. "Ah, Mara. I thought about what you'd said and decided that the next batch of remedy I whipped up would be perfect to *try out* on Sebastian. Then you can't say you didn't try to save him. You will be free and clear to move on with your life knowing that you have done all you can to bring him back. No guilt. No remorse."

"No," I gasped. I stumbled to the metal table and reached for the IV.

"I wouldn't do that. A half dose would turn him into a vegetable for sure. A full dose is the only chance he's got," Donavan said.

I lowered my hand and placed it on Sebastian's chest. His eyelids flickered, and under the lids I could see his eyes darting back and forth. I swallowed hard on the bile that rose in my throat.

Donavan stepped up and put his hands on the table. "It will take a week to ten days for the full effects to be known. Then we can decide whether to put him out of his misery, or of course, if he comes around, we will administer the same treatment to the others."

"You mean Juliana."

"One of which will be Juliana," he nodded, and I felt something inside me snap, a cruel streak I hadn't known existed until that moment rearing its ugly, vicious head.

"She'll never come around. She didn't love you enough to hang on, that's the reality, and you're just prolonging her agony and yours by believing you can still be together."

Donavan slammed his hands on the edge of Sebastian's table, his face a storm cloud of fury barely contained. I glared back at him, not backing down for an instant.

"You've doomed him to be nothing more than a shell of a man," I hissed. "Don't expect me to play nice anymore. Maybe instead of Juliana coming back, you should take the Nevermore shot and go to her."

Donavan's eyes widened, then narrowed. "You know nothing, Mara. You're a desperate, foolish little girl who thinks love can conquer all. It can't. I should know."

He turned to walk out of the room, but I stopped him with a single phrase. "Love is something eternal; the aspect may change, but not the essence. He will always love me. It doesn't matter *what* he is."

Donavan paused, but didn't look back. "You know nothing."

I didn't answer him, only pressed my hands to Sebastian's slowly rising and falling chest, praying that the remedy would work.

Donavan left, flicking the overhead lights off and plunging Sebastian and me into a semi-darkness, lit only by beeping machines, the silence filled by the steady drip of the IV.

I whispered into that gray light, holding onto my husband for all I was worth.

"Come back to me, Sebastian, my love, my heart. Come back to me."

Acknowledgements

This has been such an interesting journey to go back and tackle a story I wrote over five years ago. Breathing new life into it would not have been possible without the support of my very fantastic editors: Tina Winograd, Stephanie Erickson, and Shannon Page.

I would be remiss if I didn't mention those readers who never wanted Nevermore to end and regularly sent me emails to please continue. Thank you for believing in this story.

AUTHORS NOTE

Thanks for reading "Bound". I truly hope you enjoyed the continuation of Mara and Sebastian's story, and the world I've created for them. If you loved this book, one of the best things you can do is leave a review for it. Most of my books are available across all platforms, so feel free to spread the word.

Again, thank you for coming on this ride with me, I hope we'll take many more together. The rest of The Nevermore Trilogy, along with most of my other novels, are available in both ebook and paperback format on all major retailers. You will find purchase links on my website at:

www.shannonmayer.com

Enjoy!

About the Author

Shannon Mayer lives in the southwestern tip of Canada with her husband, dog, cats, horse, and cows. When not writing she spends her time staring at immense amounts of rain, herding old people (similar to herding cats) and attempting to stay out of trouble. Especially that last is difficult for her.

She is the USA Today Bestselling author of the The Rylee Adamson Novels, The Elemental Series, The Nevermore Trilogy, The Venom Trilogy and several contemporary romances. Please visit her website for more information on her novels.

www.shannonmayer.com

Ms. Mayer's books can be found at these retailers:

Amazon
Barnes & Noble
Kobo

iTunes
Smashwords

59439196R00175

Made in the USA
Lexington, KY
05 January 2017